AS HIS FRIEND LAY DYING . . .

Nate tensed his arms and legs, then tugged on the lance with all of his strength. To his amazement, the shaft came out easily, so easily he lost his balance and fell onto his buttocks. He flung the spear to the ground, then wiped his blood-soaked hands on the grass.

Sitting Bear was in terrible torment. He grunted, closed his eyes, and bent in half.

Drawing his knife, Nate stood and ran to the Ute he'd shot. The man wore leggings, and Nate swiftly cut strips of buckskin to use for bandages. Holding them in his left hand, he raced back to his friend and frantically attempted to stop Sitting Bear's life fluid from gushing forth. All his efforts were unavailing. The buckskin strips became drenched. Nate stood, about to cut more, when the drumming of hooves arose to his rear. Whirling, he was stunned to discover another Ute bearing down on them. . . .

4

WILDERNESS

BLOOD FURY

David Thompson

LEISURE BOOKS NEW YORK CITY

Dedicated to . . .
Judy, Joshua, and Shane.
And to Sign Talking Eagle,
who recorded it for posterity.

A LEISURE BOOK®

March 1991

Published by

Dorchester Publishing Co., Inc.
276 Fifth Avenue
New York, NY 10001

Printed in the United States of America.

Chapter One

Nathaniel King heard a twig snap, and froze. All around him was the majestic scenery typical of the Rocky Mountains in the month of August. Caps of gleaming snow crowned the towering peaks that ringed the valley in which he was hunting. Cottonwoods, aspens, and pine trees grew in profusion along the banks of the narrow stream meandering from north to south. Ink-black ravens soared lazily high above his head. Sparrows chirped in a thicket to his left. And somewhere directly ahead, hidden in the undergrowth, was the black-tailed buck he'd been stalking for the better part of two hours.

The strapping 19-year-old crouched and scanned the densest vegetation for his quarry. If he was right, if he'd learned the lessons taught by his grizzled mentor properly, then the buck should be there. Deer usually spent a hot after-noon hidden in the shade, where they could rest safe from predators until they ventured out in the cool of the evening to forage in earnest.

Nate's gaze strayed to the stream, which gurgled not more than a yard to his right, and he caught a glimpse of his reflection. His buckskins fit his broad shoulders and muscular frame loosely, allowing for adequate ventilation and unrestricted movement. An eagle feather bestowed on him by a noted Cheyenne warrior was tied securely to his long black hair, the quill pointing skyward. Slanted across his chest was a powder horn and a bullet pouch, and tucked under his brown leather belt were two flintlock pistols, one on each side of the buckle. On his left hip, nestled snug in its sheath, was his butcher knife.

A crackling sound issued from the brush in front of him.

Nate's green eyes narrowed as he probed for movement. Always look for a hint of motion against the backdrop of plant life, Shakespeare had instructed him. Now he put the teaching to good use, and spied something 20 feet away moving from east to west.

He raised the rifle clasped firmly in his hands, the heavy Hawken he'd obtained in St. Louis from the brothers of the same name who were just beginning to earn a reputation as makers of superb guns, and sighted on the vague form. He saw a flash of brown, but couldn't identify the game as the buck he sought, and he certainly didn't want to shoot something else by mistake. Especially a grizzly bear.

The animal halted and snorted.

Nate had heard such sounds before, and always from deer or elk. He was confident he'd found the buck, and he took a bead on a small opening in the undergrowth located a few yards from it. If he made the shot, he'd be able to transport enough meat to the cabin to last for two weeks, even allowing for the fact there were three mouths to feed counting his. He thought of how easy acquiring food had been back in New York; all it took was the correct amount of money and a person could eat whatever they desired. But in the wilderness the difference between a full stomach and starvation often hinged on the squeeze of a trigger or the twang of a bowstring. Since his wife and best friend were eagerly awaiting his return with fresh meat, he didn't intend to miss.

For the longest time nothing happened. The creature stayed put, apparently in no great hurry to get anywhere. A pair of robins flew into a tree above it.

The strain of holding the Hawken steady produced moderate pain in Nate's shoulders. He estimated five minutes had gone by before the thing finally stepped closer to the opening. Just a little bit farther, he mentally noted, and his patience would be rewarded.

Tentatively, as if sensing an element in the forest was amiss, the animal edged westward.

At last Nate had an unobstructed view, and there stood a magnificent buck sporting a 12-point rack. He held his breath and aimed between its eyes, which were locked on him, then squeezed the trigger.

The rifle didn't fire.

Baffled, Nate glanced down at his rifle to discover he had failed to cock it in his excitement. He hastily remedied the mistake, and looked up to find the buck on the move. Alarmed that he was about to lose such choice meat, he discarded all caution and plunged into the underbrush in pursuit.

The deer darted deeper into the timber.

Nate ran at his top speed, battering limbs aside with his arms and making enough noise to spook an entire herd of buffalo. He came to the opening and paused to survey the forest. Elation coursed through him when he spied the black-tail 60-feet away in the middle of a clearing, gazing over its shoulder in his direction, apparently more curious than afraid. Instantly he whipped the Hawken up, took a fraction of a second to line up the shot, and squeezed the trigger.

At the loud retort the buck started to turn, but the ball caught the animal in the left eye before it could take a stride. The impact jerked its head forward and the animal stumbled to its knees, tottered, and fell on its right side.

Nate was already running toward his prize. There was always the chance the deer might rise and bolt, and the last thing he wanted to do was chase the buck for miles and miles until it dropped for good. He drew his right pistol as he closed. When still 15 feet away he realized another shot wouldn't be necessary after all.

A dark crimson pool formed a halo around the buck's head and antlers. A neat hole now existed where its left eyeball had been, and its tongue protruded from between its lips.

Smiling in satisfaction at his marksmanship, Nate wedged the pistol under his belt and halted. He'd left his horse and the pack animal several hundred yards to the north in a stand of pines, so his first priority should be to reclaim them before any wandering Indians came by.

Pivoting, Nate hastened off. He returned to the bank of the stream and paused to enjoy a refreshing sip off cold water, then straightened and was about to continue when his oversight checked him in midstep.

Would he never learn?

He grinned as he reloaded the Hawken, wondering how long it would be before he automatically did so after every shot. Although he'd been on the frontier for almost five months, he still neglected on occasion to reload immediately. One day, he mentally noted, the mistake could cost him his life.

From deep in the woods came the hoot of an owl.

After replacing the ramrod, he trekked briskly northward, invigorated as much by the crisp mountain air as by his success at hunting. Feeling supremely happy, he began humming the tune to "Home, Sweet Home," a song written by John Howard Payne.

A large yellow and black butterfly flew past his face.

Nate gazed at the nearest peaks, thinking of his wife and the joy they had shared during the month and a half they'd been married. He'd learned more about women in that brief span than in all the years before the wedding. The thought made him laugh. How would he refer to a short Shoshone ceremony presided over by his wife's father as a wedding? All he'd done was promise to protect her, to treat her kindly, and to stay with her in good times and bad, and just like that they were united in matrimony.

Well, not quite.

There had been a little matter of giving her father a horse. In effect, as he saw it, he'd bought her, and the idea still rankled him. He knew that many trappers bought Indian women for a season or longer. He also knew Indian warriors customarily offered horses and other valued possessions to the fathers of the brides-to-be. In his estimation such a practice rated as a notch above outright slavery, and he disliked both.

Winona didn't mind, though.

That aspect of the practice amazed him. Indian women actually *wanted* to be purchased. They considered it to be a great honor. If a man wanted a woman for his wife and didn't offer to pay, she'd be insulted.

Nate shook his head and chuckled. How strange and wonderful life in the wild could be! If he ever returned to civilization, perhaps he would write a book on his adventures as so many of those who'd ventured West had done.

He soon reached his horses, and proceeded to lead them back to the clearing. His mare, a frisky animal he'd purchased in New York City, became skittish as they neared the spot where the buck lay. Not until he came within sight of his prize did he discover the reason, and the sight filled him with consternation. He halted, uncertain whether he should fire or flee.

A panther was astride the black-tail.

Nate had never seen one of the big cats up close. Ordinarily they took great pains to avoid humans, and would run at the first glimpse of a man or woman. They were also deathly afraid of fire. Their other habits were generally unknown to the majority of trappers because they were so reclusive. Some Indians believed seeing one was a good omen.

This one appeared to have no intention of leaving. Light brown in color, it measured six feet from the tip of its nose to the end of its twitching tail. Its rounded head was fairly small for its size, but the teeth displayed when the cat growled definitely weren't.

Nate raised the rifle. He reasoned the panther must be either very hungry or very old, or both, and decided to avoid killing it if at all possible. His mentor, Shakespeare McNair, had impressed upon him the Indian view of staying wildlife: Never kill any animal unless it was absolutely necessary.

The fierce cat snarled and swiped a paw at the intruder.

"Go away!" Nate shouted. "That's my meat!"

A feral hiss was the response.

Nate took a few paces, seeking to frighten it off, but both horses halted and refused to budge despite firm tugs on his part. Frustrated, he led them off to the east and securely tied both to the jutting branches on an enormous log. "That should hold you," he said, and cautiously made for the clearing once more.

The panther was still there. It had taken a bite out of the buck's neck, and now greedily lapped at the blood flowing onto the ground.

Resolved to recover the deer at all costs, Nate advanced steadily. As before, the cat glared at him and growled. Nate trained the Hawken on its head, never breaking stride.

For a few moments the cat held firm, its lips curled back to expose all of its wicked, tapered teeth, its eyes flashing a raging hatred. Then it rose and swiftly sped to the southwest in prodigious bounds stretching 15 feet or more. The vegetation swallowed the cat, leaving an unnatural stillness in the air.

Nate beamed and walked to the carcass. He'd saved the meat! Wait until he related the story to Winona and Shakespeare. To be on the safe side, he waited several minutes before attending to the skinning, his eyes surveying the woods in case the panther should think twice about leaving the meal.

Not so much as a leaf stirred.

The owl vented another hoot, closer this time.

Satisfied he was out of danger, Nate pulled his knife and squatted. He placed his rifle behind him, rolled the buck onto its back, and set about skinning it. Since the cat had already torn the neck open, he didn't bother with bleeding the carcass. Instead, he first cut a slit from the anus to the head, beginning between its rear legs and slicing upward. He wisely avoided puncturing the stomach and intestines.

Next, to prevent the contents of the esophagus, if any, from contaminating the meat, he tied a string around it. He did the same with the anus. His hands were coated with blood and gore, so he sat down and wiped them on the grass while admiring his handiwork. Shakespeare had taught him well.

Nate gazed at the sky, calculating the amount of time required to complete the job. By all rights, after he removed the heart, liver, and other organs, he should hang the deer from a stout limb to let the blood drain completely and give the air a chance to cool the body. He figured there were eight hours of daylight remaining, at least. If he let the buck hang for a couple of hours, he would be able to leave the valley and clear the ridge to the east before nightfall. Since he was a full day's ride from the cabin, the sooner he started, the better he would like it.

The owl hooted a third time.

Rising to his knees, Nate leaned over the black-tail, then remembered a fact Shakespeare had taught him about owls. They were nocturnal birds of prey and rarely were abroad during the day. How odd that one should be flying about in the early afternoon.

Then it hit him.

What if the cries were being made by something else?

Or, more precisely, *someone* else?

Intuition tingled the hairs at the nape of his neck and he spun, reaching for the Hawken, already too late because at the east edge of the clearing stood an Indian warrior armed with a bow, an arrow set to fly.

Chapter Two

Nate instantly threw himself to the right, holding the rifle next to his chest as he rolled over and over. Amazingly, the shaft never struck him, and he surged to his feet, bringing the Hawken up, prepared to return fire.

Only the Indian hadn't released the arrow.

The warrior nodded and spoke a few words in an unknown tongue.

Perplexed, Nate shook his head to indicate he didn't understand. He didn't know what to make of the situation. If the Indian had wanted to kill him, he'd most certainly be dead. But if the warrior had friendly intentions, why point the shaft at him?

Again the man tried to communicate, speaking longer this time.

Nate didn't know enough yet about the various tribes to be able to determine which ones individuals belonged to at a mere glance, as Shakespeare could do. He had no idea if the man in front of him was a Shoshone, Crow, Cheyenne, or Arapaho. The warrior wore leggings and moccasins and had a knife on his right hip. There were no distinguished marks, such as paint, on his face or body, and his hair was unadorned.

Of one fact Nate could be certain. The Indian wasn't a Blackfoot or Ute. Any member of either tribe would have shot him on sight. Of all the Indians inhabiting the Rockies and the Plains to the east, none caused more trouble for the trappers. Both tribes hated all whites.

The warrior glanced at the buck, then at Nate. He slowly let up on the bowstring, easing the tension, then lowered the bow to his side. A tentative smile creased his thin lips.

Reassured by the man's behavior, Nate likewise let the rifle fall to his waist, although he kept a finger on the trigger. "Who are you?" he asked. "Do you speak English?"

Now it was the Indian's turn to shake his head.

Nate didn't give up hope. Winona had taught him enough Shoshone to enable him to engage in a conversation without fear of being misunderstood. He tried that language now, but the effort proved unavailing. At last he resorted to sign language, letting his hands do the talking, and saw the warrior smile.

Almost all of the tribes relied on the silent language that had been passed down from generation to generation from their ancestors in the distant past. The origins of sign were lost in antiquity, and no one knew how the language had become so universal in extent, but its effectiveness was indisputable. Sign language enabled Indians from different tribes, who might live hundreds of miles apart and have virtually no customs in common, to establish an immediate rapport.

Of all Nate's accomplishments since heading west, he was most proud of his grasp of sign. He'd spent countless hours learning the proper movements of the hands and fingers, first under the tutelage of his late Uncle Zeke, then under Shakespeare and Winona. Just a few days ago the frontiersman had complimented him on his ability. He now told the warrior that he came in peace, that he was hunting for meat for the table and nothing more.

The Indian slid the arrow into a quiver on his back, then responded by revealing his name to be Sitting Bear.

"From which tribe do you come?" Nate asked with his hands.

"I am Crow."

Nate breathed a sigh of relief. The Crows and the Shoshones were two of the friendliest tribes in the entire territory. They befriended whites regularly and were implacable enemies of the Blackfeet and the Utes.

Sitting Bear's fingers flew. "What is your name?"

There were no Indians signs that would adequately translate his English name, so Nate disclosed the Indian name bestowed on him by the same Cheyenne who had given him the eagle feather. "I am Grizzly Killer."

The Crow blinked. "Are you the same Grizzly Killer who was at the big gathering of whites during the last Blood Moon?"

Blood Moon was the Indian way of referring to July. "I am," Nate responded.

Sitting Bear seemed impressed. "And are you the same Grizzly Killer who killed the Bad One?"

"Yes," Nate admitted, wondering how the warrior knew about the incident at the rendezvous involving a rogue trapper and his band of cutthroats.

"I am happy to meet you," Sitting Bear said with his hand. "I camped with a band of Bannocks nine days ago. They were at the big gathering and told me all that happened."

So that was it, Nate thought. "I am happy to meet you," he dutifully stated. "But why did you point an arrow at me?"

"For that I am most sorry. I did not know if you would be a friend or an enemy. Some whites believe all Indians are enemies and shoot us without warning."

"I only shoot Indians if they try to shoot me," Nate assured him.

Sitting Bear came closer and pointed at the black-tail. "I heard a shot and came to see who it was." He admired the deer for a moment. "You will have much meat."

Remembering the many lessons Shakespeare had imparted on Indian etiquette, Nate knew what he had to do. "I would be pleased to share some of the meat with you."

"I could not accept," Sitting Bear signed, although his expression betrayed his interest. "Even though my family has not tasted deer meat in three moons."

Nate smiled and walked over to the warrior. "I insist you take some of the meat. There is more than I can possibly use."

The Crow considered the offer for a few seconds, then looked up. "I will accept your kindness if you will agree to share my lodge tonight."

"How far is your lodge?"

Sitting Bear pointed to the south. "A mile from here on the west bank of the stream."

Nate hesitated. He wouldn't be able to make

it back to the cabin tonight anyway, so why not accept? If he rode out at first light, he'd be home shortly after dark tomorrow. "I would be happy to," he signed. "I'll stay at your lodge tonight, but I must leave in the morning."

"You honor me," Sitting Beat said solemnly. "My friends will not believe that so great a warrior has stayed with my family."

The compliment made Nate feel uncomfortable. He had yet to accustom himself to the frank manner in which Indians discussed everything. They were invariably direct and to the point, and they never practiced idle flattery. Evidently the news of his encounter with the Bad One was spreading rapidly by word of mouth around the campfires of the whites and the Indians. At the rate things were going, soon he'd be as widely respected and feared as Shakespeare. "How many members of your tribes are here?" he asked to change the subject.

"My wife, my two sons, and my daughter."

"Your family is here alone?" Nate inquired in surprise. The Central Rockies were the hunting grounds of the Utes, and for any Crow to travel into the region was extremely dangerous.

"Yes."

"What about the Utes?"

Sitting Bear shrugged. "We had to come. There was no choice."

Nate looked around. "Do you have a horse?"

"No."

"I must go get mine. Would you watch my buck while I am gone?"

"Yes. I will guard it as if it was my own."

Gripping the Hawken by the barrel, Nate hurried toward his animals. It was his understanding that only the poorest of Indians didn't own horses, and he wondered why Sitting Bear hadn't simply stolen a mount from another tribe. Horse stealing was a common pastime. Special raids were frequently conducted expressly for that purpose, and those warriors who succeeded were esteemed as brave men. Not to mention rich. Horses, to Indians, were conspicuous evidence of affluence.

He found the mare and pack animal munching contentedly on grass, and in no time at all he was back at the clearing and standing over the buck. "Will you give me a hand hanging this up?" he asked. "I have rope in one of my packs."

"We can take the buck to my lodge," Sitting Bear suggested. "My wife has made berry juice, and my sons will take care of your horses."

Nate liked the idea. This was his first contact with the Crows, and he was curious to learn more about them, to see how they differed from the Shoshones. "Let us go," he said with his hands.

Together they lifted the buck onto the pack animal and strapped it down tightly. Nate swung into the saddle, took the lead in his left hand, and nodded for his newfound friend to show him the way.

"Is it true you are close to Carcajou?" Sitting Bear queried, glancing over his shoulder to catch the reply.

"Yes," Nate sighed. Carcajou was the name by which Shakespeare was known far and wide among the various tribes. The word itself was French, Nate believed, and referred to the fierce animal otherwise called the wolverine.

Sitting Bear used his hands as he walked, the bow slung over his left shoulder. "I met him once years ago. He is a white man whose word can be trusted."

Nate started to respond, but he realized the warrior wasn't looking at him. He focused on the surrounding trees, searching for the panther or any other threats. The likelihood of the big cat returning was slim, but in the forest it never paid to take chances.

For ten minutes they wound southward. Sitting Bear demonstrated an uncanny knack for finding passages through the thickest brush, usually by following the narrowest of animal trails. The trees thinned out, and ahead appeared a clear strip adjacent to the stream.

Nate rode to the edge of the water. Across the stream, nestled at the edge of the woods on the far side of the field, sat Sitting Bear's lodge. Smoke curled lazily upward from the ventilation opening at the top. A woman and a young girl were seated outside the lodge, working on a buffalo robe. Two boys, both in their teens, were honing their skill with bows and arrows near the trees.

Sitting Bear raised his right arm and hailed them in his native tongue, then glanced at Nate. "Come," his hands stated. "Meet my loved ones."

Nate waited for the warrior to enter the water, then urged the mare forward. The stream had a depth of two feet at its deepest points and was only five feet in width. He crossed easily and reined up on the far bank.

The family ran out to meet him. All four halted a few yards off and regarded Nate with amazement and, in the case of the mother, a trace of fear.

Sitting Bear indicated their guest and launched into an extended speech in Crow. The quartet listened attentively, with repeated stares directed at Nate.

For his part, Nate was amused by their reaction but tactfully maintained a solemn face. He noticed the boys were keenly interested in his rifle. The little girl, who wasn't any older than ten, smiled at him the whole time.

At length Sitting Bear concluded and turned. His hands and arms did the talking as he explained his comments to Nate. "I told them about our meeting and let them know you are the great Grizzly Killer. I told them you have kindly offered to share your meat with us, and that they must all be on their best behavior."

Nate faced them and addressed them in sign language. "I am most happy to meet all of you."

The woman nodded nervously, the girl giggled, and the boys couldn't seem to take their eyes off the Hawken.

"Let me introduce them," Sitting Bear said, coming around in front of the mare. He touched each member of his family as he went from one to the other. "My wife is Evening Star. Our daughter is Laughing Eyes."

"Hello," Nate said aloud.

The Crow paused, his features reflecting his pride. "And these are my sons, Strong Wolf and Red Hawk."

Both boys grinned self-consciously. The taller of the pair, Strong Wolf, said something to his father in their own language.

"He wants to know if you will allow him to shoot your rifle," Sitting Bear disclosed. "But he is too shy to ask you himself."

"I would be happy to have him fire it," Nate replied, and was about to compliment his host on having such a fine family when the mother suddenly pointed to the east and cried out in alarm. Twisting in the saddle, he discovered the reason.

A herd of 25 or 30 buffalo had crested a rise
seven hundred yards distant and were pounding
directly toward the camp.

Chapter Three

Nate turned the mare, then used sign language to explain his purpose to Sitting Bear. "Hold my pack horse and I will turn the herd," he proposed.

"Be careful," the Crow replied, taking the proffered lead.

The small herd raised tendrils of dust behind it as the huge beasts drew closer.

About to ride off, Nate paused when an idea occurred to him. He glanced at his host. "Would your family like a buffalo or two?"

The suggestion brought a wide smile to the warrior's face. "We would be much in your debt," he responded.

"Have Evening Star sharpen her knives," Nate advised, and goaded the mare into the stream again. He crossed quickly and rode to intercept the bison.

Although the majority of the great brutes migrated from the high country to the Plains early in the spring, there were always those

hardy animals who seemingly preferred the
higher elevations and stayed in the mountains the
year round. They grew as large as their counter-
parts below, with the males standing over six feet
high at the shoulders and weighing upwards of
two thousand pounds, and were similar in every
other respect except for the fact their coats were
shaggier.

Few animals were as numerous as the buffalo.
On the Plains their numbers were estimated to
be in the millions. A single herd could take days
to pass a specific point. And of all the wildlife
existing west of the Mississippi River, the bison
were most essential to the Indian way of life.

Every tribe utilized the buffalo to some extent.
Hides were used for clothing. Robes, moccasins,
leggings, shirts, dresses, belts, and even under-
clothes all came from treated skins. Lodge
furnishings, riding gear such as saddle blankets,
hackamores, and hobbles, and various tools and
utensils were constructed from various parts of
the beasts. Knife sheaths and shields were
manufactured from rawhide. Bowstrings were
made from bull sinew. Even the buffalo's dung
came in handy; chips were burnt as fuel.

Nate had encountered bison before, and he
held them in great respect. With their broad,
massive heads sporting horn spreads of up to
three feet, and the fiery temperament of the bulls
when aroused, they were formidable game. They
were also hard to kill unless the person doing the hunting knew exactly where to hit
them. He'd heard about trappers who'd put 15
balls into a single bull, yet the animal had refused
to drop.

And here he was trying to turn a herd of 30.
Shaking his head in astonishment at his own

audacity, Nate pondered how he could best achieve his goal. Riding straight at them in the hope of diverting them to either side would be an exercise in futility as well as certain suicide. A shot might do the job, but he must time it perfectly and hope the lead bull wasn't in a belligerent mood.

The thundering hooves of the onrushing bison became louder and louder.

Nate spied a mammoth male at the head of the herd and made toward it. The mare responded superbly; she'd participated in a buffalo hunt with him once before and wasn't fearful. He held the rifle and the reins in his right hand, then drew a pistol with his left.

Already the brutes had covered two hundred yards.

Almost as an afterthought, Nate speculated on what could have spooked them. Buffalo were notorious for standing their ground against their natural enemies such as wolves and panthers. Normally, they even refused to flee at the sight of men, Indian or whites. If Nature had given them the intelligence and ferocity of the grizzly, the buffalo would have long since driven all two-legged creatures from their domain.

The flat land worked in Nate's favor. He had plenty of room to maneuver and could outrun them if the need arose. To the north lay the forest; to the south a level field. He didn't particularly care which way they went, just so they turned aside from Sitting Bear's camp.

On they came, the largest animals in North America, their bulky bodies rising and falling rhythmically as they ran.

Nate extended the pistol, counting off the yards separating him from those tapered horns. He waited until there were only 50, and fired.

For a few seconds the buffaloes acted as if they hadn't heard, and then they started to swing to the south.

Elated at his success, Nate went to rein up when the mare suddenly stumbled and went down, throwing him from the saddle. He thrust his hands out to brace the impact, and winced when a searing pain lanced up his right arm. Tumbling end over end, he wound up flat on his back, dazed, staring at a cloud overhead.

What in the world had happened?

He rose onto his elbows and saw his horse rising. Behind her were a series of holes with openings a foot wide. Badger burrows. Concerned the mare might have broken a leg, he shoved to his feet and grabbed the reins.

From his rear arose the drumming of the buffaloes.

Nate glanced over his right shoulder and was stunned to discover the herd had resumed its original course and was a mere 20 yards distant. His guns had flown from his hands when he fell, and he frantically searched the high grass around him.

The Hawken lay not four feet away.

Hauling the mare after him, Nate lunged and scooped up the rifle. He swung toward the herd, cocked the hammer, and prayed the weapon wouldn't misfire. In an instant he sighted on the lead bull and pulled trigger.

For a heart-thumping second the herd came on rapidly, a living wall of tough sinew and iron determination, their nostrils flaring, their humped shoulders bouncing.

Nate recoiled, expecting to be trampled and gored, and seized the mare's mane in a desperate bid to escape. He saw the foremost bull go down in a disjointed jumble of flashing legs and whipping tail, sliding to a stop within inches of his moccasins, and the rest of the herd split into two groups, half bearing to the left, half bearing to the right. The pungent scent of them filled his nose, and dust obscured everything. He held onto the mare with all his might and listened to the rumbling din as the beasts passed him by. The very ground shook.

In moments the herd had left him behind.

Coughing and waving his left hand to dispel the choking dust, Nate took several strides to the west. Had he done it? Or were the bison still bearing down on the lodge? He scarcely breathed until he glimpsed the herd, reunited and racing to the southwest, well clear of the camp.

Relief washed over him and he voiced a cry of triumph. His temples still pounded, and when he held his arm out his fingers trembled. But he was alive! Fully, wonderfully, alive, tingling in every fiber of his being. He spun in a circle, laughing heartily, then walked to the dead bull and stared down at its huge head and dark eyes. "You almost got me, big fellow," he said by way of a compliment.

Shouts rent the air from the direction of the lodge.

Turning, Nate saw the Crows running toward him, the mother carrying the girl in her arms. He grinned and indicated his trophy.

Sitting Bear reached him first. He uttered a whoop and began prancing around the buffalo, waving his bow overhead.

Nate chuckled, tempted to join the warrior.

Strong Wolf and Red Hawk were next, and they promptly joined their father in the victory dance, yelping like coyotes as they leaped and whirled.

Girlish laughter announced the arrival of Evening Star and Laughing Eyes. They stood to one side, observing happily, and the mother gave Nate a friendly look.

Proud of his accomplishment, Nate hefted the Hawken. If not for the rifle, he'd be dead. The reliable weapon had saved his skin once again, and the thought prompted a decision. There were some frontiersmen who took to calling their rifles by pet names. He'd always considered the practice rather foolish until that very moment. Old Reliable was a fitting name for a rifle, and from that day on he would refer to his Hawken as exactly that: Old Reliable. He couldn't wait to tell Shakespeare the news.

The Crows were still celebrating wildly.

Nate lowered the rifle, his right wrist brushing against the pistol wedged under his belt. He abruptly recalled his other flintlock and turned, scanning the field. It had to be there somewhere. But what if the flailing hooves of the buffaloes had pounded it to bits?

Sitting Bear stopped dancing and walked over. He said a sentence in Crow, then resorted to sign language. "Every word they say about you is true. You are the bravest man I have ever met."

"Thank you," Nate replied, still scouring the grass.

"My family will always treasure this day, and the story of your deed will be passed on to my grandchildren and my great-grandchildren. I will also record the events on a hide for all future generations to see."

Nate stopped looking and smiled at the Crow. "You honor me too much. I only did what I had to do to stay alive."

"You are still young. You do not yet realize the

gift the Great Mystery has given you."

"What gift?"

"The gift of courage."

Nate had never regarded himself as exceptionally brave. He smiled and gestured at the trampled field. "I need your help."

"Anything we can do for you, we will."

"I lost one of my pistols," Nate began to explain, and the warrior cut him off.

Sitting Bear barked instructions to his family, and every one of them immediately devoted themselves to searching for the missing flintlock.

Nate resumed hunting, thinking of how close-knit Indian families were, how they stuck together and were supremely devoted to one another. He'd yet to witness or hear about a single instance of a child disobeying a parent. By comparsion, many of the families in the cities had succumbed to the severe stress of city living and were rife with animosities. Many children treated their fathers and mothers with outright disrespect. There were some who claimed the crime in the cities was due to the breakdown of discipline and parental guidance. Perhaps they were right.

Strong Wolf gave a yell and raised his left arm.

Nate beamed when he laid eyes on the flintlock. He hurried to the youth's side and took the gun in his hand, inspecting it carefully. The pistol wasn't damaged. He guessed that the grass and weeds had cushioned it from the hooves, and he chuckled at his good fortune as he slid the barrel underneath his belt.

"Is it broken?" Sitting Bear inquired.

"No." Nate glanced at the eldest son. "Thank you for finding it."

The boy pointed at the bull. "You have given us enough meat to last a month. I am glad to help you."

Sitting Bear squinted up at the sun. "We must get busy if we are to finish by nightfall. Now we have a buffalo and a buck to skin and strip."

"I am ready when you are," Nate offered.

"We will take care of both," Sitting Bear stated. "You can rest while we work."

"We will work together," Nate insisted.

"As you wish. We will go get all the knives, rope, and utensils we need."

"I will stay here."

The Crows hastened toward their camp, chatting excitedly among themselves.

A sensation of extreme fatigue seized Nate, a belated reaction to his brush with death, and he wished he could curl up on the ground and take a nap. To keep busy, he methodically went about reloading the Hawken and the flintlock.

The mare took to nibbling on the sweet grass.

He idly gazed at the lodge, and saw the family bustling about in the vicinity of the lodge. They were decent people, those Crows, and he was glad he'd met them. He hoped he could prevail on Sitting Bear to travel to his cabin. Winona would be grateful for the company, and Shakespeare genuinely liked making new acquaintances.

Nate stretched and stared at a lofty peak to the south. What were his parents and brothers doing at that very moment? he mused. Did they miss him? Were they still mad that he'd departed New York City so unexpectedly? Or had they forgiven him and wanted him to return?

His peripheral vision registered movement.

Nate shifted to the east, looking toward the rise over which the buffaloes had appeared, and there, seated on a brown stallion, was an Indian warrior.

Chapter Four

For a moment Nate stood still, recovering from his surprise. The man had on a buckskin shirt and leggings and carried a lance. He couldn't determine if the warrior was a Crow or from another tribe, and he wondered how long the Indian had been watching him. A glance over his shoulder confirmed that Sitting Bear had yet to start in his direction. He faced the warrior and waved.

The Indian didn't move.

Puzzled and curious, Nate stepped to the mare and vaulted into the saddle. He gripped the reins tightly and galloped toward the figure.

Immediately the warrior wheeled his horse and disappeared over the crest.

Nate rode hard until he came to the rise, then reined up. Below was a gradual slope and a wide meadow hemmed in by dense forest. The Indian was nowhere in sight. Mystified, he leaned on the pommel and surveyed the woods. Why had the man run off? Was the warrior friendly or hostile?

He waited several minutes, hoping the Indian would show himself.

The woods were quiet, the meadow serene.

So much for trying to establish contact, Nate reflected, and rode back toward the bull. Although the man hadn't made any threatening gestures, Nate was bothered by his presence. He'd learned to regard everyone he encountered in the wilderness as a potential enemy until they demonstrated otherwise.

Joking and laughing, the Crows were finally returning.

Nate reached the buffalo first and dismounted. He debated whether to inform them and decided withholding the news might prove disastrous later.

"Where did you go?" Sitting Bear signed when he was still a dozen feet off.

"I saw a warrior on horseback."

The disclosure brought a worried expression to the Crow's face. He gazed eastward, then swept the south and north horizons. "Do you know which tribe he was from?"

"No."

Evening Star was clearly troubled. She addressed her husband apprehensively.

Sitting Bear responded softly, his forehead creased, in deep thought.

"If you are worried, I can help you move your camp," Nate offered.

"What good would it do? A competent tracker would find us in no time. I say we stay where we are until morning, then we shall move," Sitting Bear stated. "We cannot leave until we are done with the butchering anyway, which will not be until after dark."

"If you are sure," Nate said.

Sitting Bear nodded.

They set about skinning the buffalo. Nate marveled at the skill and efficiency of the Crows. Both Sitting Bear and Evening Star wielded their knives with expert precision, knowing exactly where to cut to speed the process along. They only stopped once, after an incision was made in the abdomen.

Nate watched in fascination as the warrior laid his bloody knife on the ground, then reached into the abdominal cavity and pulled out a handful of intestines.

"Would you like some?" Evening Star queried.

"'No, thank you," Nate answered, his stomach churning, slightly nauseated by the grisly, pulpy mess of entrails.

The Crows each took a portion and began eating ravenously, chewing and smacking their tongues, their chins dripping wet. The little girl giggled as she ate.

Nate pretended to be interested in a distant mountain. He'd been told by Shakespeare that Indians usually ate buffalo intestines and the brains at the site of a kill because neither could be preserved, but the foreknowledge hadn't braced him for the reality.

Far above the mountain a bald eagle soared.

After five minutes the family concluded their snack and resumed skinning the shaggy brute.

Nate noticed Laughing Eyes grinning up at him, her cherubic features caked with gore, and he thought about the child Winona and he planned to have at the first opportunity. He realized that his wife undoubtedly would teach the youngster to partake of intestines too, and he nearly burst into laughter envisioning how his parents would react to such a scene.

Compared to life in the Rockies, New York City was an alien world.

The flickering red and orange flames cast dancing shadows on the interior of the warm lodge. Curling wisps of smoke wafted up and out the ventilation flap, and the aroma of the cooking food permeated the air.

Nate gazed at the pot in which the venison stew boiled. Constructed from the buffalo's paunch, it was supported next to the fire by four thick, straight limbs lashed together at the top to form a peak.

Evening Star monitored the progress of the meal attentively. She kept the stew heated by regularly dropping in heated stones taken from around the fire, and stirring vigorously. Earlier she had added wild onions and turnips to the concoction.

Nate couldn't wait to tear into the food. Butchering the bull and the black-tail had been hard work, and combined with the other events of the busy day had left him fatigued and famished. He glanced at Laughing Eyes, who stood beside her mother, then at the boys, who were seated across from him on Sitting Bear's right.

The lodge inside was typical of those Nate had seen. A brightly painted inner lining covered the lower third of the sides. Hanging at various points on the sides were three bows and quivers, a shield, a medicine bag, and parfleches— rawhide bags used to hold everything from food to herbs. The bedding was rolled up at the rear, and other possessions were scattered along the base.

"We can never thank you enough for the gift

of the buffalo," Sitting Bear reiterated yet again.

"I only wish I could have shot another one for you," Nate said.

"Will you consider staying with us tomorrow?"

"I would like to stay, but I must take the deer meat home," Nate explained.

The warrior shrugged. "I understand."

"May I ask you a question?"

"Of course."

"What are you doing here by yourself? Where is the rest of your tribe?"

"North of here three days' travel. I will rejoin them after I collect the feathers."

"What feathers?"

"Those of the eagle."

Nate reached up and touched his own. "Do you shoot them to bring them down?"

Sitting Bear blinked. "Who would kill a bird to get just its feathers?"

Acutely self-conscious of having demonstrated his ignorance of Indian customs, Nate quickly tried another query. "Do you take the feathers from nests?"

"No, I take them from the eagles."

Nate grinned. "And what are the eagles doing while you are removing their feathers?"

"They try to esape, but cannot."

"Do you catch them in traps?"

"No, with my bare hands."

"How is such a feat possible? Surely the eagles try to claw you."

The warrior nodded. He held out his left arm and tapped a two-inch scar above the wrist. "An eagle did this when I was fourteen."

Nate looked at Strong Wolf and Red Hawk. "Do your sons help you?"

"No. They are not old enough. Soon Strong

Wolf will accompany me, and I will teach him the way that was handed down to me by my father."

"But you still have not explained the reason your family is here alone. It would have been safer to bring friends along, other families who could help out in times of need."

"The shame is mine, so I must do this alone. My family came with me because they love me."

Shame? Nate almost requested an elaboration until he recollected the advice his mentor had given concerning the private affairs of others: Never pry.

"Would you care to hear my story?" Sitting Bear asked.

"Yes."

"Very well." The warrior sighed. "Two moons ago I was one of the happiest men in the Crow nation. I had counted twenty-seven coup and owned fourteen horses. All the young men respected me, and the chief asked my opinion in our councils. My family never went hungry. The Great Mystery smiled on my life."

Nate leaned forward, hanging on every word.

"And then the tragedy occurred," Sitting Bear signed. "One day a hunter reported seeing signs of an Arapaho raiding party near our village. The chief believed the Arapaho were there to steal our horses, and he decided to post guards at night to protect them. I was chosen to stand guard on the second night."

Strong Wolf and Red Hawk both frowned.

"I had worked hard that day," the Crow went on. "I foolishly let myself become tired, and that night I could barely keep my eyes open. For as long as I could I tried to stay awake, but eventually I fell asleep. The Arapahos must have been watching, because as soon as I closed my eyes, they struck. I was hit on the back of the head, and the next thing I knew, one of my friends was shaking my shoulder and shouting at me for letting the Arapahos get the better of us."

Nate looked at Evening Star and noticed her sad countenance.

"The raiders got away with thirty-nine of our horses," Sitting Bear related. "Not only that, but one of those fish-eaters, probably the same one who knocked me out, took the five feathers I had in my hair."

"Fish-eaters?"

"My people never eat the creatures of the rivers and lakes."

Nate nodded his understanding. By calling the Arapahos fish-eaters, Sitting Bear had handed them the ultimate insult.

"I was ashamed in front of my whole tribe," the warrior related. "It was bad enough I let the horses be taken, but the Arapahos added to the insult by leaving me alive. They were letting everyone know of their contempt for my people."

It took Nate a few seconds to grasp the warrior's meaning. By not killing Sitting Bear, the Arapahos had shown they viewed all Crows as less than men. The raiders were saying, in effect, that they weren't worried in the least about the fighting prowess of the Crow warriors and didn't dream the Crows worthy of counting coup on.

"I could not hold my head up anymore," Sitting Bear said. "The younger men mocked me. The chief no longer wanted me at the councils. I made amends as best I could by giving away all of my horses to some of those who lost animals in the raid, but it was not enough to restore my honor."

Now Nate understood the reason the family didn't possess horses. He also comprehended the

significance of the quest for new eagle feathers.
"So you plan to replace the feathers that were
stolen?"

"Yes, and then I will wage war on the Arapahos
and recover the same number of horses that were
taken."

"All by yourself?"

"Yes."

The forceful sincerity of the reply impressed
Nate. "But you will not stand a chance alone."

"I lost them alone. I will recover them alone."

"You will be killed."

Sitting Bear squared his shoulders. "At least
I will die with honor and my family will not be
shunned by my people."

Nate knew all about the importance of honor
and proper behavior to an Indian. Insults must
always be redressed and taboos must never be
violated. But the task Sitting Bear had set for
himself was impossible.

"Tomorrow I will start on the road to reclaim-
ing my manhood," the warrior vowed.

Just then Evening Star walked over bearing
bowls of stew. She dutifully distributed one to
each of the men, then brought on cakes and a
previously boiled flour pudding to which dried
fruit had been added to give it a delicious taste.

Nate ate with relish, savoring every morsel.
Few words were spoken by anyone; they were all
too famished. Except for the noises they made
while eating and the crackling of the thin
branches fueling the fire, the only other sound
was the whispering of the northwesterly breeze
against the lodge. So it was that midway through
the meal they all distinctly heard the patter of
heavy pads from outside followed by the guttural
growl of a large bear.

Chapter Five

Strong Wolf and Red Hawk were up and to their bows in a flash. They each grabbed arrows from one of the quivers and turned.

Sitting Bear addressed them sternly while slowly rising. He walked to the side and retrieved his own bow and an entire quiver, then stepped toward the front flap.

Although the very notion of tangling with another bear bothered Nate, he grabbed his rifle and stood. He'd already experienced harrowing encounters with two grizzlies, and if he never saw another bear as long as he lived he'd be happy.

The mother said a few words in Crow.

Silence reigned outdoors. The bear had ceased growling and moving about.

Nate cocked the Hawken and halted to the right of the flap, which was closed but not tied. He caught the warriors' attention and made the sign for "Now?"

"Wait," Sitting Bear said, listening with his left

ear pressed to the liner.

The sound of loud sniffing filtered inside, and part of a paw appeared underneath the flap.

Instinctively, Nate crouched and pointed the barrel at the center of the flap. If the bruin came through the doorway, they'd be trapped. There wasn't another way out.

Sitting Bear motioned with his right arm, signifying not to fire. He crouched and drew his hunting knife.

Perplexed, Nate watched in fascination. The bear paw eased further inside, revealing black hair and claws over an inch long, and he expelled his breath in relief. It was a black bear, not a grizzly! Even though the former were dangerous when cornered, they weren't in the same class with their fierce cousins, the mightiest carnivores on the continent and the scourge of Indians and whites alike.

Grinning at a private joke, Sitting Bear reversed his grip on the knife, holding the weapon by the blunt edge of the blade, and raised it overhead. He waited until the full foreleg of the bear poked within, then brought the hilt down with a resounding thump.

A bestial bellow erupted from the startled black bear and the paw was yanked from view.

Nate laughed as he heard the bruin beating a rapid retreat into the forest at the rear of the lodge. It crashed through the underbrush like a bull gone amok.

"Perhaps I should have invited the bear for supper," Sitting Bear signed, and his entire family joined in a chorus of general mirth.

Chuckling, Nate eased the hammer down and returned to his seat. He resumed eating, and in no time at all had finished the meal. No sooner had he swallowed the last morsel than Evening Star brought seconds of everything. Despite being almost full, he tackled the second portions with as much enthusiasm as he had the first, knowing that it was considered an insult for a guest not to eat every bit of food that was offered.

After the meal the family sat around and discussed every topic under the sun, from the habits of the wildlife to the state of affairs among the Crows and the rest of the tribes inhabiting the Rocky Mountains and the Plains.

Nate learned a great deal about their customs and beliefs. He learned there were approximately seven thousand members of the Crows nation, and that about four thousand were women. Due to the high mortality rate of the men, who daily risked their lives while hunting, on raids, or in defense of their villages, there was a chronic shortage of suitable husbands. The same state of affairs existed in other tribes as well.

Some of their customs were quite intriguing. He discovered it was a serious breach of conduct, punishable by the harshest of penalties, for a parent to strike a male child. Children were taught the correct way of doing things, and then received constant encouragement to always do good and obey all tribal laws. Rarely did the Crows have problems with their offspring.

The subject of chiefs came up, and Nate posed a question when he heard Sitting Bear mention one by the name of Long Hair. "Why does he have such a name when all Crows have long hair?"

"Because none have hair as long as his. When last I knew, it was twice as long as you are tall."

Nate knew better than to doubt the statement, even though he was skeptical. "Does he tie it around his waist so he can walk?" he asked.

"No. He wears it folded at the back of his head. They say his hair has never been cut, never trimmed, since he was a baby. I have talked with him a few times, and I can tell you I have never seen such hair as his. It is the color of fresh snow and as soft as the best robes."

The topic drifted to the subject of buffalo and beaver. Sitting Bear mentioned that he'd noticed declining numbers of both in recent years and attributed the drop to the presence of white men.

Nate grinned and shook his head. "How can you blame us? First of all, there are not more than a few hundred whites in the whole territory. Second, the Indians kill far more of both than the trappers and the hunters."

"All I know is that before the whites came, there were many beaver in all the streams. Now there are fewer, although there are still a lot. As for the buffalo, once every valley in the mountains was home to small herds. Now a person can ride for hours without seeing a single one."

"I would not worry about it," Nate commented. "There are enough beaver to last for a hundred years, and the buffalo will never die out."

The warrior adopted a solemn air. "I pray not. If the buffalo ever die, then all the Indians will fade away too. The Crows, the Arapahos, the Cheyenne, the Sioux, and the Kiowa will all become as dead grass and blow away on the wind."

"You forgot about the Blackfeet and the Utes."

"They will never die off."

"Why not?"

"They are too mean to die."

Nate laughed, and they went on to discuss the benefits the white man had bestowed on the

Indians, such as guns, better knives, and tin pots and pans. Toward midnight the conversataion finally wound down. The children and Evening Star were already asleep under buffalo blankets when Nate turned in. He positioned his blankets close to the door in case he had to relieve himself.

Slowly the fire died down until only the embers were sparkling and gave off occasional sparks.

Lying on his back with his head resting on his hands, Nate gazed at the conical ceiling and mused on the bizarre twists and turns of outrageous Fate. If anyone back in New York City had ever told him he'd one day share a meal with a family of Crows and enjoy every minute of their company, he'd have thought the person to be insane. He looked forward to prevailing on Sitting Bear to visit his cabin. The idea of staying over another day to observe how the warrior obtained the eagle feathers appealed to him, but the obligation of getting meat to his wife and friend took precedence.

Eventually Nate dozed off. He dreamed of lovely Winona, of her dark tresses and unfathomable brown eyes, and imagined he felt the warmth of her pliant body next to his. Then he also imagined he heard soft footsteps and assumed she had gone outside to attend to the call of Nature. Sluggishly, filled with drowsiness from his head to his toes, he imagined that he opened his eyes and gazed at the entrance.

The cruel visage gazing in at him was not his wife's.

Instantly the face vanished, and Nate grinned at the foolishness of his dream. Then he heard Sitting Bear snoring, and he suddenly realized he wasn't asleep. The face had been really there! Shocked, he sat up and seized the Hawken, swiveling to cover the flap.

The hide hung motionless.

Nate shook his head vigorously, striving to wake up. He blinked and glanced at the sleeping Crows, then at the vestige of the fire that scarcely illuminated the interior. None of them had so much as stirred. If there had been someone at the door, one of them was bound to have heard. He decided he must have imagined the incident, after all, and was about to lay back down when his ears registered the muffled tread of a solitary footfall.

Shoving to his feet, Nate inched to the flap and waited for the noise to be repeated. He wondered if he was all excited for no reason. Maybe the bear had returned, and in his dreamy state he'd envisioned the bear's head as that of a human. It was the middle of the night, after all, and few men, even Indians, were abroad after the sun set.

There were no other sounds for over a minute.

Nate pursed his lips, debating whether to retire or investigate. He was tempted to inform Sitting Bear, but refrained because he'd feel like an idiot if there was no one out there. If he had any brains, he reasoned, he'd simply secure the flap and go back to bed. But he couldn't.

A cool breeze caressed his left cheek as Nate emerged into the enveloping darkness. He moved to the right and squatted to prevent anyone who might be lurking out there from taking a bead on his silhouette against the background of the lighter lodge.

From off to the southeast an owl hooted.

Nate was reminded of the hoots he'd heard earlier. He'd forgotten to ask Sitting Bear if the Crow had made the calls. Inching forward, he eased onto his elbows, then flattened, searching in all directions for the nocturnal prowler.

The leaves in the woods rustled from the breeze, and in the west a coyote howled.

Oblivious to the passage of time, Nate stayed immobile. He couldn't go back to sleep until he knew for sure. The prospect of having his throat slit while he slumbered was a tremendous incentive to stay alert. He heard insects, and the faint, hideous scream of a panther, but no more footsteps and there was no hint of movement in the forest.

He twisted and focused on the field. A quarter moon on high cast a feeble radiance on the landscape. He could see the mare and the pack horse, hobbled 30 feet away, moving slowly along while they ate.

Think! Nate chided himself. If there was an Indian spying on the camp, the man must be nearby. He recalled the warrior he'd observed on the rise, and speculated that the same Indian must be the culprit. After five more minutes elapsed and the night refused to yield its secrets, he opted to crawl to the south. If he hid in the high grass, he might be able to catch the warrior in the act.

A bug flew out of nowhere and hit him in the left cheek.

Nate recoiled, then grinned grimly. If he wasn't careful, he'd give himself away. In ten yards he reached a patch of waist-high vegetation and slid into concealment. He turned, his movements methodical, trying to shake the grass as little as possible, and faced the lodge.

Now all he had to do was wait.

Fatigue gnawed at his consciousness, dulling his awareness despite his best effort to remain fully awake. He placed his forearms on the hard earth and propped his chin on top. Something crawled over his left hand, but he ignored it.

The moon arched higher on its westward passage.

Nate's eyelids drooped. He wondered if he was being foolish, if the whole incident might not be the product of his overactive imagination. Those comfortable blankets awaiting him in the lodge were more and more tempting as each minute went by. Sighing, he put his palms on the grass and tensed to rise.

There was brief motion to the west.

All drowsiness evaporated. Nate gripped the rifle and squinted, his eyes riveted to the front of the lodge. The only way someone could get to the Crows was through the entrance. All he had to do was keep watching the flap, and sooner or later the person would appear.

Seconds later someone did.

Nate distinguished a hunched-over figure gliding toward the doorway. He warily pressed the rifle to his right shoulder, then hesitated. Should he fire, when there was a remote possibility the nighttime stalker could be friendly, or issue a challenge?

The figure drew tentatively nearer to the flap. There wasn't much time to decide. Nate reflected on what Shakespeare McNair would do in the same situation, and cocked the Hawken once more.

Unexpectedly, a second figure materialized, treading on the heels of the first. Then a third and a fourth came into view, all strung out in a line as they crept around the lodge.

There was no doubt the Crows were about to be attacked. Four against one weren't the best odds, but Nate couldn't let those men get inside.

He rose to his knees at the same moment the leading form moved next to the flap, and with the profound hope his wife wasn't about to become a widow he aimed as best he could and squeezed the trigger.

Chapter Six

The sharp retort of the Hawken was punctuated by a shrill screech, and the figure near the flap toppled backwards. Nate crouched and drew his right pistol, and the motion saved his life.

One of the attackers returned fire.

Nate heard the ball whiz past overhead even as he extended the pistol and shot at the second form. The target staggered against the lodge, then straightened and bolted for the sanctuary of the forest.

The other pair also fled.

"Damn you!" Nate bellowed, and burst from cover. He slipped the discharged flintlock under his belt and pulled out its mate, but there was no sense in trying another shot.

All three figures reached the trees and dashed into the dense undergrowth.

Nate was tempted to loose a parting shot anyway. The folly of wasting his last ball disuaded him, and he turned to the one he'd shot.

Shouts arose in the lodge. Sitting Bear snapped

commands, and Laughing Eyes cried.

Exercising extreme caution, Nate stepped over to the man on the ground. As he'd suspected, it was an Indian. He nudged the warrior with his right toe and received no response.

Suddenly the flap swung open and out barged Sitting Bear, an arrow notched to his bow. He almost tripped over the body, halting in amazement.

"They're gone," Nate said, knowing his friend wouldn't comprehend the words but hoping the message would get across. For added emphasis he gestured forcefully at the woods.

The Crow nodded, then knelt and examined the casualty. He muttered a sentence in his own tongue that ended with a familiar term. "Ute."

Nate stiffened and swung around to cover the trees. Where there were four Utes, there might be more. He deliberated whether to pursue them, but the matter was taken from his hands before he could make a decision.

Strong Wolf and Red Hawk emerged. Their father spoke to the eldest and pointed to the west. Without a word they sprinted off.

Nate wanted to ask a question, yet had to refrain because the darkness would obscure his hand movements. He saw his host seize the Ute and start dragging the man inside. As the flap parted, light played over the two Indians. He guessed that Evening Star had rekindled the fire.

Not a sound came from the forest.

Should he stay out and guard the lodge or join Sitting Bear? Nate wondered, and chose the latter. Squatting, he darted inside, and stopped short at finding the Ute blocking his path.

The enemy warrior would never stalk another foe. The ball had hit him squarely in the forehead between the eyes and burst out the rear of his cranium. His dark eyes were wide and lifeless. He wore leggings and moccasins, but no shirt, and a knife was tucked into the top of his pants. Amazingly, his left hand still clutched a tomahawk.

"This is a Ute," Sitting Bear disclosed in sign language.

"I know," Nate said. "There were three more. I think I hit one of them." He paused. "Perhaps you should call your sons back before they run into those three."

"No. My sons must learn the art of war and there is no better teacher than experience."

"They could be killed."

"Life is but the pathway to death."

The profoundly philosophical response wasn't the answer Nate anticipated. He tried another tack. "But they're just boys."

"True. Boys who are eager to become men, and among my people manhood is attained only after coup has been counted for the first time."

Nate glanced at the mother, thinking she might give him moral support, but she hadn't been paying attention. Her gaze rested on the Ute. Her arms were around Laughing Eyes, who had stopped crying.

"We were fortunate there were only four of the skunk-eaters," Sitting Bear stated, and looked at Nate. "And once again you have done my family a great service. How did you know they were out there?"

"They woke me up."

"Truly you have the senses of a wildcat," Sitting Bear remarked. "When we return to my village, I will tell all of my people about the greatest white man I have ever met."

Nate didn't know what to say. He appreciated the compliment, although the blatant exaggeration bothered him. If things kept going the way they were, soon he'd have reputation to match Jim Bridger's.

Evening Star spoke for a minute, pointing repeatedly at the body.

"She says she does not want the Ute left in here all night to soil the air," Sitting Bear translated. "I must haul him out after you are done."

"Me?"

"Yes," the Crow said. "You killed him, so by all rights his hair is yours."

Nate looked at the body. Revulsion filled him at the thought of slicing the warrior's scalp off. He'd done the horrid deed before, but it became more difficult to do each time.

"Is something wrong?" Sitting Bear asked.

"I grow weary of taking scalps," Nate confessed.

"You have that many?"

"More than I will ever need."

Sitting Bear shook his head in amazement. "I have known one other man who had more scalps than he needed, and he was an old chief who had counted at least one coup for every one of his seventy-two years."

"That is a lot," Nate agreed, placing his hand on the hilt of his knife. He wished there was a way he could avoid scalping the Ute, and he grinned at an idea that popped into his mind. "May I ask you a question?"

"Certainly."

"Please bear with me, because I do not yet know all the ways of the Crows. In return for the kindness you have shown me, I would like to give you a gift."

"You have already given us the buffalo."

"I know. But the bull was for your whole family. This would be a personal gift from me to you."

"What is this gift?"

"The Ute's scalp."

The warrior's mouth fell open. "I have never heard of such a thing."

"Would you accept such a gift?"

Sitting Bear assumed an intently thoughtful expression. He reached out and touched the Ute's hair, then glanced to his right at the string of 14 scalps already adorning the teepee. "You are very kind in making such an offer, but I cannot accept. The Ute's hair is yours. You must be the one to scalp him."

"I was afraid you'd say that," Nate said in English, and knelt beside the dead man's head. He leaned the Hawken against the side and slowly pulled his knife out.

Evening Star spoke to Laughing Eyes in a stern manner, emphasizing her point with firm gestures.

Stalling, his stomach slightly queasy, Nate looked at the warrior. "What does your wife say?"

"She is explaining that Laughing Eyes must never again cry in times of danger. Did you hear her?"

"Yes."

The Crow frowned. "Such behavior is not tolerated. Women, as well as men, must learn to be brave. Are white women brave?"

Caught off guard by the question, Nate had to think of all the white women he knew. "In their own way they are as brave as the men, although very few of them have ever taken part in war or been in fights."

"Our women do not fight either, unless the village is being attacked. Then they all become as fierce as rabid wolves."

Nate girded himself for the task at hand.

"The Utes do, though," Sitting Bear said.

"Do what?"

"Let their women fight. That is because they are less than animals and have no knowledge of the proper ways of men and women. Some women even go on raids."

The revelation startled Nate. What if the other one he'd shot had been a woman?

"I have a friend who killed a Ute woman in battle," Sitting Bear went on. "He said she fought as well as any man and he was sorry to have to take her life. Now her hair is one of his prized scalps and he would not part with it for a dozen horses."

"How nice," Nate commented, and gripped the top of the dead Indian's hair. He inserted the tip of his knife into the skin at the hairline and proceeded to neatly remove the grisly trophy.

"Well done," Sitting Bear stated when the job was done. "I have not met many whites who know how to take hair, but you do."

"Thank you."

"Would you like my wife to wash it for you?"

"If she would be so kind," Nate sighed, and gladly handed over the hair when Evening Star came over in response to her husband's instructions.

The patter of rushing feet arose outside, and a moment later Strong Wolf and Red Hawk dashed excitedly into the lodge. Both talked at once. Sitting Bear held his right arm aloft, quieting them, then posed a series of questions that they dutifully answered.

"What happened?" Nate asked when the warrior paused.

"The Utes are up to their old tricks. There were four horses hidden west of here and they made good their escape."

"What will you do now?"

"Stay."

"But they might return."

"I cannot leave until I have five feathers to replace those that were stolen," Sitting Bear declared.

"Are five feathers worth the lives of your loved ones?"

"My mind is made up," the Crow stated obstinately.

Nate reclaimed his rifle and moved to one side as the boys attended to stripping the corpse and then dragged it from the lodge. He moved close to the fire and held his hands over the flames, enjoying the warmth. Sometime ago Shakespeare had explained to him the concept of Indian honor, and detailed how in some tribes a man would do anything to regain prestige once he had fallen from social grace. In a way Nate felt sorry for Sitting Bear. The disgrace of having let the precious horses be stolen was more than the poor man could bear, and now the Crow was willing to sacrifice his family rather than endure the disgrace.

What should he do? Nate asked himself. Stay and assist the warrior or head on home? He wanted to return to Winona quickly, but he couldn't bring himself to desert Sitting Bear in the man's hour of need.

The Crow came over. "I apologize if my words seem hard. My family and I have discussed this issue and we are all of one mind."

"I understand."

"Since you will probably leave early tomorrow, I thought I should tell you again that we are grateful for all you have done."

"Who said I am leaving?" Nate responded.

"You plan to stay?"

"I would like to see how you catch eagles with your bare hands."

The warrior's eyes narrowed. "Is that the only reason?"

"Yes."

"You are not obligated to us in any way."

"I know," Nate said, and remembered the question he had to ask. "Was that you today hooting like an owl?"

"About the time you shot the black-tail?"

"Yes."

"That was me. When I heard your shot, I believed you might be a Crow so I called to you as an owl would. We often call to each other by imitating the owl. When there was no answer, I knew you were either a stranger or an enemy. That is why I approached you with my arrow ready to fly."

"Perhaps you can teach me the call sometime."

"Gladly." Sitting Bear turned to walk off. "We should get sleep. Tomorrow will be a busy day."

"Should I take the first watch?"

"What?"

"We should take turns doing guard duty until daylight," Nate proposed. "I will go first."

The Crow grinned. "There is no need. The Utes will not be back tonight."

"How do you know?"

"I know," Sitting Bear stated enigmatically, and moved to the bedding he shared with his wife.

The boys returned bearing the clothing, weapons, and other personal effects belonging to the slain Ute. They deposited the items in front of Nate.

"Give these to your father," Nate told them. "I have no need of them." He reluctantly walked to his blanket and lay down, listening to the family discuss his gifts, and positioned the rifle next to his side. With a hostile band of Utes roaming the area, he wasn't about to go to sleep. Instead, he rolled on his back, propped his head in his cupped hands, and reflected on the whims of Fate. Here he was, about to participate in an eagle hunt, when if he possessed any intelligence whatsoever he'd ride out at first light. As the Crow had said, tomorrow would undoubtedly be a busy day.

Just so it wasn't his last.

Chapter Seven

Whispered conversation brought Nate awake, and he opened his eyes to find golden rays of sunlight streaming in the open flap. Startled, he sat up and clutched the Hawken. He couldn't believe he'd fallen asleep! Outside the lodge were Strong Wolf and Red Hawk, both engaged in sharpening arrows. He looked behind him and saw Sitting Bear, Evening Star, and the little girl by the fire.

"The new day has begun," the warrior signed.

Nate numbly nodded and ran his left hand through his hair. He had no idea when he'd finally dozed off, but he felt as if he'd only slept for an hour or so.

"We have tried to be quiet so as not to wake you," Sitting Bear disclosed. "I did not know you are such a late riser."

Late? Nate peered through the doorway again and saw the tip of the sun peeking above the eastern horizon. What did the Crow consider to be early? he wondered, and rose sluggishly. He went outside, smiled at the boys, and walked into the forest to relieve his bladder. The crisp morning air invigorated him, and he swung his arms back and forth to get his circulation going. Birds chirped lustily on all sides, greeting the dawn in their own inimitable manner. The avian choir assured him there were no Utes in the area. He propped the rifle against a tree, attended to business, and returned to the lodge.

Strong Wolf glanced up and his hands flew. "My father has told us you are going with him today. It is good. He is a brave man, but he should not be out there alone."

"I agree," Nate concurred, and entered.

Evening Star beckoned him. In her right hand she held several small, round cakes.

"Would you like to eat before you leave?" Sitting Bear queried.

"Yes," Nate said, joining them. He took a seat and gratefully accepted the cakes.

"We have a two-hour trip to the eagle peak," Sitting Bear revealed. "If all goes well, we can be back here by midday."

Nate placed the cakes in his lap to pose a question. "Is that two hours on foot?"

"Yes."

"Then I suggest we ride to save time."

"We could save a little, perhaps," the Crow said, "but most of the journey is uphill over very steep terrain. The horses would only slow us down and we would be forced to leave them a mile from our destination. While I thank you for the offer, your animals would be safer if we left them with my family."

"Whatever is best," Nate stated, and dug into his breakfast. In five minutes he consumed the cakes and enjoyed a cup of blackberry juice Evening Star provided.

Sitting Bear spoke to his wife, then slung a leather pouch over his left arm, grabbed his bow, aligned his quiver on his back, and started for the flap. "I am ready if you are," he announced.

"Wait," Nate said, and quickly checked the rifle and both pistols to ensure they were loaded. Once done, he walked to the entrance and grinned. "Lead the way."

They exited, the warrior in the lead. He took the time to speak to both of his sons, then gestured and led the way to the northwest.

Nate stayed a few yards behind the Crow, moving as silently as he could, his eyes constantly roving from side to side as he alertly scanned the undergrowth. His host set a rapid pace that he easily matched, and they covered several miles without incident.

The forest eventually ended at the base of a sparsely covered hill, which they negotiated. Then they started up a high mountain. On the craggy heights above were bighorn sheep, white dots against the brown of the cliffs the animals frequented.

Nate saw Sitting Bear slow and peer intently at a thicket to their right. He halted when the Crow did, and he was all set to inquire about the reason for the delay when the warrior stooped and lifted a fair-sized stone. Puzzled, Nate kept silent.

Sitting Bear suddenly hurled the stone into the middle of the brush, and out darted a large rabbit. It picked up speed swiftly. In a fluid, practiced motion the Crow whipped an arrow from the quiver, notched the shaft, elevated the bow, and took a fraction of a second to aim.

Nate watched in fascination. The rabbit bounded all out, and he didn't see how anyone could hit such a streaking target. He heard the humming vibration as the string was released, and glimpsed the flashing arrow. To his amazement, the rabbit abruptly tumbled end over end, dead before it came to a stop, the shaft jutting from its twitching body.

The warrior hastened to recover the animal and came back grinning happily. He slung the bow over his right shoulder and nodded at the peak far above them.

"Why did you kill it?" Nate asked.

Sitting Bear stuck the exposed portion of the shaft under his left arm and answered with his hands. "To use as bait. Come. We have a long way to climb."

They did exactly that, going steadily upward. The slope, at first, was gradual and dotted with trees and patches of shrubs.

Nate tilted his head and spied a solitary eagle soaring on the currents to the south. The distance was too great to determine if it was a golden eagle or a bald eagle. Both were numerous in the Rockies, as were many varieties of hawks.

The climb became more arduous the higher they ascended. Fields of enormous boulders had to be traversed and occasional crevices skirted. Sheer cliffs were bypassed. The sun rose steadily, warming even the rarefied air at the upper elevations.

A layer of sweat caked Nate's skin by the time they came to an incline spanning a hundred yards in length and twice that distance in width. Short alpine grass covered the ground.

Sitting Bear stopped and turned. "We are here."

Nate gazed uncertainly at the grassy stretch. "This is where you will catch the eagles?"

"Yes." The Crow headed for the center of the tract.

Perplexed, Nate followed. He scanned the heavens for eagles, but saw none. On another mountain to the north, near the summit, was a large herd of elk making for the lower regions.

Slowing, Sitting Bear studied the area ahead. He voiced an exclamation in Crow and walked to a shallow depression, where he knelt and began feeling the surface with his fingers extended.

Nate placed the rifle stock on the ground and simply observed, at a loss to explain the Indian's behavior. He thought about Winona, and passionately wished he was with her instead of on a forlorn peak many miles away. In all fairness, he mentally noted, he had only himself to blame. He was the one who had craved deer meat when there were other types to choose from. The lake near his cabin abounded in fish. There was also plenty of elk and small game in the neighborhood of his homestead. Even a small herd of buffalo. If he'd settled for a continued diet of fish or a different game animal, he'd be snug and warm in his own home where he belonged.

The warrior chuckled and began tugging at something. Moments later he succeeded in lifting a three-foot-square latticework constructed from thin limbs.

Amazed, Nate stepped nearer. The limbs had been woven tightly together to form a sturdy platform on which there rested an inch or two of soil topped with grass. Perfect camouflage, he realized, and grinned at the ingenuity displayed. Under the covering was a circular pit, its sides braced by a layer of flat stones.

Sitting Bear shoved the latticework to the left and looked at Nate. "This pit was dug by my father's father. There is another over there," he revealed, and pointed at another slight depression ten feet off. "Conceal yourself within. Soon an eagle will come. If I am fast enough, I can get all five feathers I require from one bird. If not, we will be here a while."

"Is there anything I can do to help?"

"Just do not make any noise. Not even a sneeze. And whatever you do, be sure not to bump the covering. Eagles have great eyesight and can see a blade of grass tremble from a mile up."

Nate knew that to be an exaggeration, but he refrained from debating the point. He moved to the spot indicated and succeeded in removing the cover to a second pit. A glance back disclosed his companion positioning the bait at the edge of the trap by jamming the bloody tip of the arrow that transfixed the rabbit into the soil. Nate eased down onto his buttocks, pleased to find there was enough room to sit up. The rifle went between his legs. By poking his fingers into the lattice-work, he grasped the cover and slid it over him, leaving an inch gap on the side facing the Crow's hiding place so he could view whatever transpired next.

Sitting Bear dropped into the first pit and covered himself. He aligned the top to leave a gap for his arms next to the rabbit.

The simplicity of the technique appealed to Nate, and he marveled yet again at the adaptability of the Indians to their environment. They had met Nature on less than equal terms and bested her. Whether they were hunting buffalo or obtaining feathers, whether they were selecting medicinal herbs or edible plants, they demonstrated an affinity for the wild that the whites couldn't hope to match. Oh, there were a few white men who had lived among the Indians long enough to be their equals, but in general the Indians had learned to live in harmony with the wilderness while the white race sought to conquer it.

Time went by slowly.

Nate made himself as comfortable as he could. A layer of gravel covered the bottom, and he was tempted to lift the covers and tear out some grass by the roots to use as cushioning. To do so would spoil the trap, however, so he bore the minor irritation in resignation. He leaned against the side, his eyes on the rabbit, his mind adrift in reflections of his childhood in New York City. Sometimes, especially in periods of inactivity, he missed his family and civilization.

He dwelled on the lovely woman he'd planned to marry, Adeline Van Buren, and hoped she'd secured another eligible beau, someone her father would approve of. No doubt she had. With her natural beauty, wit, and charm, she could take her pick of any man in New York. He'd never quite understand what she'd seen in him. In his eyes, she'd been a goddess and he her supplicant.

Who would ever have thought that he would give up a Venus like Adeline to marry an unaffected Indian woman who was as far removed in her manners and customs from the ways of polite society as the sun from the earth? Truly the whims of circumstance and design were beyond comprehension.

Nate began to feel sleepy, and he struggled to keep his eyes open. He didn't want to miss the moment when an eagle first took the bait. Try as he might, though, the lack of rest took its toll and his leaden eyelids closed.

A peculiar fluttering sound reached his ears.

Instantly Nate's eyes snapped open. A loud swishing filled the air, and out of the blue plummeted a diving bald eagle, its terrible talons

pointed downward, its wings held erect as it
dived for the kill. With bated breath he saw the
mighty bird grab hold of its prey, and at that very
moment a pair of sturdy arms surged from under
the adjacent latticework and firm hands seized
its legs.

The eagle promptly strained upward, its wings
beating powerfully, voicing an unusually weak
chittering cry from so magnificent a creature.

Sitting Bear straightened, the covering on his
shoulders, his sinews rippling as he fought to
restrain the bird. He managed to grip both its
legs in his left hand and plucked at its white tail
feather with his right.

At last the eagle understood what was
happening and twisted, trying to peck the Indian
in the head and neck. Its own wings prevented
the bird from craning its neck far enough.

Nate stood, tossing the covering to his pit
aside, and scooped up his rifle. He wanted to
assist his friend but had no idea what to do.

The Crow managed to tear out four feathers
and was working on the fifth. His left hand
slipped, and the eagle turned even further and
snapped at his left shoulder. He ducked to avoid
the bird's wicked beak, then wrapped his fingers
around a fifth white plume.

Enraged to the point of being berserk, the eagle
flailed and thrashed savagely, its wings striking
the warrior again and again. It was able to tear
its left leg free, and like a striking rattlesnake it
lanced one of the biggest beaks in the bird
kingdom, a beak that could shred the toughest
of flesh, at its tormentor.

Nate gazed in horror as the eagle tore into
Sitting Bear's face.

Chapter Eight

Nate surged out of the pit and raced toward the Crow. "Sitting Bear!" he cried out, unable to fire because of the proximity of the bird.

Voicing a shrill shriek, the eagle suddenly took wing, speeding skyward with the dead rabbit still clutched in its steely talons.

The warrior pressed his left hand to his face. Blood trickled over his fingers as he gazed at the departing creature, a wry smile on his lips.

"Are you all right?" Nate inquired urgently in English, temporarily forgetting himself. He quickly rephrased the query in sign language.

Sitting Bear nodded absently, his eyes brimming with triumph. He lowered the hand to reveal a nasty cut three inches long, from just under his left eye down to his chin.

"That eagle almost took your eye out," Nate declared. "What do you have to be so happy about?"

Smiling wider, Sitting Bear extended his right arm and slowly unfolded his right hand. Resting in his palm was the fifth feather.

"You did it!" Nate gestured excitedly. "Now you have all the feathers you need."

The warrior collected all five plumes and climbed onto the grass. He stared up at the eagle, still visible but receding rapidly, and spoke in the Crow tongue.

Nate was delighted at the success of their quest, for more reasons than one. Now they could return to the lodge, and before too long he would be on his way home. If it wasn't for the threat of the Utes, all would be well.

"I thanked the eagle for the gift of its feathers," Sitting Bear explained after a minute. "My first task is done. Next I will recover the horses stolen by the Arapahos."

"Are there other warriors who will go with you?"

"No. Until I reclaim my honor, my friends shun me."

"They do not behave like friends."

Sitting Bear shrugged. "It is the Crow way." He gingerly ran a finger along the slash he'd sustained. "I will have a scar," he commented proudly.

"We should wash it at the first opportunity or it might become infected," Nate noted.

"Evening Star will apply herbal medicine. She is a skilled healer."

Nate tilted his neck and spied the dwindling form of the great bird. "I learned an important lesson today."

"What lesson?"

"I would rather have a feather given to me than pluck one myself."

The Crow laughed heartily.

After covering the pits, they commenced the

descent, the flush of triumph and the pull of gravity conspiring to hasten their pace so that they reached the bottom in much less time than the climb had taken.

"I have an idea," Nate signed as they were crossing the hill side by side. "Why not bring your family to my cabin and spend time with us? My wife will be delighted, and I know your wife would not mind."

"True. Women are more social than men. But I must think on it."

"Why?"

"Because if we visit you, my quest to restore my standing in my tribe will be delayed."

"What harm can a few days do? Besides, I have another friend staying with me whom you might like to meet."

"What is the name of this friend?"

Nate grinned. "Carcajou."

The warrior pondered the news. "Yes, I would like to see Carcajou again. Perhaps we will come with you. But we have a problem."

"What?"

"We travel very slowly without horses to pull our lodge. My sons and I must do the hauling while Evening Star carries our daughter and parfleches. You would be delayed getting back."

Nate stared straight ahead, debating whether to offer his animals to transport the lodge. He abruptly halted when he spotted figures moving in the trees below. There were men on horseback riding toward the hill. He grabbed the Crow and yanked him flat.

"What is it?" Sitting Bear signed.

Nate simply pointed. He recognized the riders as two Indians. The foremost warrior appeared to be inordinately interested in the ground. A tracker, Nate realized, and the man was smack dab on their trail.

"Utes," Sitting Bear said.

"Two of those from last night," Nate speculated. What could have happened to the third? Had his ball eventually killed the man?

"They have not seen us yet."

Twisting, Nate scoured the slope for a place to take cover. There were a few trees off to the left, and a low cluster of brush to the right. Neither was ideal, but under the circumstances there was no alternative. He nudged the Crow and indicated the three trees. "We should make our stand there."

"Lead the way."

Nate turned, placed the rifle in the crooks of his elbows, and crawled rapidly southward. He glanced repeatedly at the forest, marking the progress of the Utes. The pair rode out of the woods at the same time he reached the trees, whose trunks were no thicker than his thigh and afforded scant protection, and rose to his knees.

Sitting Bear crouched behind the next tree and drew an arrow from his quiver as he unslung his bow.

Advancing at a surprisingly leisurely rate, the Utes ascended the hill. The one at the rear was talking animatedly.

"They believe we are hours in front of them," Sitting Bear related. "Once the tracker sees our return tracks, they will know we are here."

Nate estimated the duo would pass within 20 yards of their position, and started to state as much when he remembered there was no sign motion for the word "yard." He modified his statement. "They will come within twenty paces of us. I will take the first man if you will slay the second."

"When you fire, I will."

Easing onto his stomach, Nate braced the barrel on the bole and waited. The lead Ute carried a lance, while the second warrior held a bow. Since Indian men could hurl a spear or shoot an arrow with uncanny speed and accuracy, he took slight comfort from the edge his rifle gave him. If he missed, there wouldn't be an opportunity to reload it; the flintlocks would be his last resort.

Onward came the warriors, the lead rider leaning over his animal's neck to better see the soil.

Nate took a bead on the first Ute's chest, his pulse quickening. He glanced at the slope, estimating the point where their return tracks had ended when they crawled to the trees, and decided to fire when the warriors were at least 15 feet from the spot.

The second Ute fell silent and idly surveyed the countryside. He stared at the mountain to the west, the mountain to the northwest, and then at the trees.

Nate's breath caught in his throat. The Utes were 40 yards off, too far to guarantee both would be killed at the outset of the impending fight. They must come closer! He remained still, well aware of the keen eyesight Indians possessed.

Displaying no alarm, the Ute strayed his gaze farther south.

Relieved, Nate grinned and adjusted the position of his left elbow.

The second Ute's head unexpectedly snapped toward the trees again and he reined up, calling out to the first man, who also stopped.

Dread welled within Nate like a bitter bile, and he cocked the Hawken in anticipation of what would happen next. Nor was he disappointed.

Gesturing excitedly, the second Ute abruptly whooped, hefted his bow, and charged. A second afterward the lead rider followed suit.

Casting caution to the wind, Nate stood and aimed at the first man. He delayed firing for several seconds, wanting to be sure, then squeezed the trigger.

Simultaneous with the cracking discharge the foremost Ute performed a remarkable maneuver. He swung down on the off side of his animal, using his left forearm and his left foot to retain his hold on the horse, minimizing the target he presented.

Nate knew the ploy firsthand, knew it would take an exceptional shot to dislodge the Indian from his perch. He lowered the rifle and drew both pistols.

Thirty yards out the second Ute was in the act of drawing his bowstring to his cheek when Sitting Bear's arrow took him high on the left side of his chest. He jerked backwards and tumbled from his mount, landing on his side, then pushed erect with the shaft jutting from his torso.

Sitting Bear stepped into the open, another arrow nocked, intent on making his next shaft the final one. He totally ignored the first Ute.

Since the tree afforded some protection, Nate stayed where he was. He lifted both flintlocks, trying for a clear shot at the leader, unwilling to shoot unless he was certain of scoring.

The tracker was only 20 yards away, his horse bearing down on the trees at full gallop, his foot and forearm the only parts of him in view.

Knowing he shouldn't let the Indian get any closer, Nate dashed from his marginal cover, racing to the west, trying for a better angle. He had managed four strides when the Ute suddenly straightened and hurled the lance. Instinctively, he ducked, thinking the warrior had thrown the weapon at him. But he was wrong.

Standing tall, exposed and unsuspecting, Sitting Bear let his arrow flash forward. With his gaze riveted on the wounded man, he never saw the slim spear that arced through the air and struck him just above the right hip. The impact spun him around. He dropped his bow and fell to his knees, his face distorted in agony, clutching at the lance.

The fury that dominated Nate's mind caused him to take a reckless gamble. Already the lead rider was swinging from sight again, and only his head and shoulders were above the horse. Nate rashly pointed both pistols and fired them together.

Twin balls bored into the Ute's forehead, and he uttered a short scream as his arms flung outward and he toppled to the hard earth.

Nate pivoted, concerned about the second enemy, but Sitting Bear's arrow had pierced the center of the man's chest and laid him out flat. Sitting Bear! He ran to his friend, who was doubled over and trembling, and squatted next to him.

The Crow looked up, grimacing, beads of sweat on his brow. He hissed a few words in his language and nodded at the Utes.

Nate placed the flintlocks down and examined the wound. The lance had transfixed Sitting Bear, with about half its length sticking out his back. Blood flowed copiously, covering his thigh and leg in red.

Gasping with the effort, the warrior moved his

hands to say two words. "Pull it."

Nodding, Nate licked his lips and moved around in front of the warrior. He knelt, seized the bloody spear in both hands, and looked into Sitting Bear's eyes. "This will hurt like hell," he stated.

Although he hadn't understood a word, Sitting Bear bobbed his chin and gulped.

Nate tensed his arms and legs, then tugged on the lance with all of his strength. To his amazement, the shaft came out easily, so easily he lost his balance and fell onto his buttocks. He flung the spear to the ground, then wiped his blood-soaked hands on the grass.

Sitting Bear was in terrible torment. He grunted, closed his eyes, and bent in half.

Drawing his knife, Nate stood and ran to the Ute he'd shot. The man wore leggings, and Nate swiftly cut strips of buckskin to use for bandages. Holding them in his left hand, he raced back to his friend and frantically attempted to stop Sitting Bear's life fluid from gushing forth. All his efforts were unavailing. The buckskin strips became drenched. Nate stood, about to go cut more, when the drumming of hooves arose to his rear. Whirling, he was stunned to discover another Ute bearing down on them—a Ute armed with a fusee.

Chapter Nine

Fifty feet separated Nate from the onrushing Indian. All three of his firearms were empty, and the knife he held was no match for the warrior's gun.

Fusees were smooth-bored flintlocks the Indians received in trade with the fur companies, particularly the Hudson's Bay firm. The barrels were invariably shortened to accommodate ease of handling on horseback. All fusees were notoriously inferior to the rifles of the trappers and mountain men, both in range and accuracy. At under 25 yards, though, they were formidable weapons.

Nate was surprised the Indian hadn't fired already. He saw the man weave as if drunk, and noticed a crimson stain on the warrior's buckskin shirt. In a flash of insight he perceived it must be the one he'd shot outside the lodge.

The Ute slowed and tried to level the fusee.

Desperately casting about for anything he could employ to defend himself, Nate saw Sitting

Bear's bow lying in the grass. He dropped the knife and scooped it up, then slid an arrow from the Crow's quiver. A hasty glance showed him the Ute had stopped and was taking aim.

During his early teens Nate had taken an interest in archery and learned the basics. He'd spent many an idle hour practicing, and learned the proper way to draw the string and sight along an arrow. After the first several months he'd been consistently able to score a hit within two or three inches of the center of the target.

Now he notched a slender shaft constructed from ash to a bowstring composed of buffalo sinews, elevated the bow, and pulled. To his consternation, the string barely moved. He looked at his adversary and saw the Ute slumped forward, the fusee pointed at the grass. Again he endeavored to pull the string back, straining his muscles to their utmost, and succeeded in drawing the sinews to his chin.

The Ute was straightening.

Nate's left arm trembled as he tried to hold the bow steady. He attempted to aim, but the tip of the shaft kept moving up and down.

Scowling in sheer hatred, the Ute lifted the fusee to his shoulder once more.

A sensation of impending doom spurred Nate to make a last, herculean effort. He brought the string all the way to his ear, held his breath for a second, and let the arrow fly.

A blurred bolt of wooden lightning leaped from the bow to the Ute. The shaft struck the Indian below his left ribs and twisted him around. He grabbed the arrow, teetered precariously, and pitched over.

Nate grasped another arrow and raced toward the warrior. He had to be sure before he could attend to Sitting Bear. As much as he disliked finishing off a helpless foe, he had no choice.

Exhibiting remarkable endurance, the Ute rose to his knees. He'd dropped the fusee as he fell, and it lay a yard to his right. With the shaft protruding from his body, he moved slowly toward the gun.

Despite himself, Nate admired the tenacity of the Indian. He nocked the second arrow as he ran, and when he came within eight feet of the Ute he halted and whipped the bow up.

Apparently hearing the footsteps, the warrior glanced at the white man. He stared at the razor point fixed on his chest and uttered a defiant challenge in his own language, shaking his left fist in anger.

Nate let the bow do his talking. This time the shaft pierced the Ute high on the right side of the chest, and the man fell without voicing another sound. Satisfied by his victory, but disturbed by the deed, Nate returned to Sitting Bear.

The Crow was almost unconscious. His eyelids fluttered like the wings of a hummingbird, and he breathed in loud, ragged gulps. Blood continued to gush from the wound.

In a frenzy of anxiety, Nate racked his brain for something he could do. If the bleeding didn't cease soon, Sitting Bear would assuredly die. Since bandages hadn't worked, he must try something else. But what?

Inspiration hit him when his eyes strayed to the trees. He tossed the bow to the earth, retrieved his knife, and sprinted to the source of the Crow's salvation. Working furiously, he hacked off and collected an armful of thin limbs, raced to Sitting Bear's side, and proceeded to make a fire. He tore out handfuls of dry grass to use

as tinder, then turned to the blaze itself. Since
the flint he normally used was in a pack back at
the lodge, he restorted to a trick he'd seen
performed by a trapper at the rendezvous. He
quickly reloaded one of the pistols and held the
gun at ground level, next to the limbs.

Nate cocked the flintlock, then packed kindling
all around it. He hesitated before squeezing the
trigger, afraid the tactic wouldn't work. A groan
from Sitting Bear reminded him of the necessity,
and he fired into the ground. Thankfully, stray
sparks ignited the dry grass on the first shot.
Elated, he bent down and nursed the initial pin-
points of flame by blowing lightly on the tinder.

It took several minutes of sustained effort, but
Nate succeeded in getting the fire going. He stuck
the pistol under his belt.

Sitting Bear was on his right side, unconscious,
his leggings drenched.

Nate waited until the fire crackled before
selecting a branch that would suit his purpose.
He gripped the outer end and slowly turned it
over and over, letting the flames char the
opposite tip. Not until it glowed bright red did
he lift the branch and turn to his companion. He
rolled the Crow over, exposed the hole, and began
cauterizing the wound, inserting the scorching
tip as far as it would go.

The grisly operation seemed to take forever.
Nate repeatedly reheated the tip. Each time the
branch touched Sitting Bear's flesh, there would
be a loud sizzling and a pungent smell. He came
close to gagging twice. Eventually the bleeding
stopped. By then the rims of the entry and exit
holes had been burnt a crisp black.

There was no rest for the weary. Nate gathered
all of his weapons, reloaded his guns, and walked

toward the horse belonging to the third Ute. The animal, a fine black stallion, had moved less than 40 feet from the spot where its rider had been slain. It nibbled at the grass, and glanced up once as Nate approached. He moved carefully so as not to spook the steed.

True to Indian custom, the horse had a war bridle attached to its lower jaw with a lark's-head knot. The rope reins dangled from its neck.

Nate slowed to a snail's pace when a yard from the stallion. "Be a good boy," he said softly. "Don't run off."

The horse paid him no attention.

Tentatively extending his right hand, Nate succeeded in grasping the reins. He patted the animal's neck to reassure it, then swung up onto the bare back. Happily, the stallion didn't resist. "Just don't buck me off," he said, and goaded the steed forward, finding the horse easy to control. Swinging in a loop, he rode back to his friend.

One of the other Ute mounts was 60 feet to the north. The last animal had strayed to the west a good 40 yards.

Nate stared at Sitting Bear, then at the horses. He thought about the sacrifice the man had made to atone for the Arapaho raid and came to a decision. Wheeling the stallion, he rounded up the others.

Only then did Nate try to revive the Crow, but without water his efforts were unavailing. He slung the bow over his left arm, then carefully lifted Sitting Bear onto the horse and held him up while climbing on behind him. Gripping the warrior around the waist, Nate headed out. He wished he could carry the weapons belonging to the dead Utes, but his arms were full as it was.

So began the long ride to the lodge. Nate was

compelled to travel slowly for fear of jarring Sitting Bear and starting the hole bleeding again. He constantly scoured the forest for additional enemies. Fortunately, none appeared.

The golden orb dominating the heavens climbed steadily higher. Low gray clouds filtered in from the west, then bigger and darker ones. The breeze intensified, becoming a brisk wind.

Nate looked over his shoulder and frowned at the sight of the blackened horizon. Roiling harbingers of Nature's elemental fury were bearing down on the woodland, and he estimated they would overtake them before he covered another mile.

As was often the case at the higher elevations in the Rocky Mountains, the storm raged across the landscape with astounding rapidity. The trappers and the Indians often remarked about the incredibly swift changes that occurred. One minute the sky could be sunny and clear; the next minute the atmosphere could be in intense turmoil. Many a hunter had found himself taken unawares by a freak hailstorm or snow shower in the middle of the summer, to say nothing of the fierce thunderstorms that shook the very earth and gave the impression the world was coming to an end.

Nate saw numerous lightning flashes, and heard the peal of distant thunder. He urged the stallion as fast as he dared, and searched for shelter. The tops of the trees were already bending, and the moist smell of rain was in the abruptly humid air. He disliked being in the midst of so many towering giants, each one capable of attracting a bolt from above. Scattered drops began to fall, and just when he resolved himself to taking shelter at the base of a trunk, he spied the cliff.

To the north, barely visible above the forest, was a high outcropping of rock. It ran from east to west and was crowned with pine trees.

Thankful to find any sanctuary at all, Nate made for the cliff. His arms were feeling the effects of the sustained strain of holding Sitting Bear on the stallion while leading the spare animals, and he looked forward to taking a break.

The forest went almost to the cliff wall. Nate paused at the edge of a narrow strip of grass bordering the base to pick where he would make his stand. More and more rain descended every second, and he blinked as drops splattered on his brow.

To the east, perhaps 50 feet away, was a spacious opening. Nate rode to it, and smiled at discovering a cavern 20 feet high and the same distance wide that extended back into shadowy recesses. He lost no time in dismounting and taking the horses inside. As he gently deposited the Crow on the dusty floor, the storm unleashed its full fury.

Lightning crackled nonstop. The attendant thunder rumbled continuously. Like the yowling of a pack of wolves, the wind howled tremendously loud. The sky became an inky canvas.

Nate knelt and watched the trees dancing as if alive. He hoped the lodge would be able to withstand the savage onslaught, and wished he'd reached it first.

Sitting Bear groaned.

A bigger problem prsented itself. What was he going to do after he got the Crow home? The warrior would be in no condition to hunt or defend his family for days, probably weeks. Nate debated whether he should stick around, and the mere thought provoked anxiety. He simply couldn't stay away from his wife for that long.

Winona would worry herself sick. There had to be an alternative, but what?

A brilliant flash lit up the cavern when a nearby tree was struck, and the resultant thunderclap startled the horses.

Nate rose and soothed them, holding onto the reins and speaking calmly. In a couple of minutes they quieted and he returned to Sitting Bear.

Gradually the frequency of the lightning strikes abated, but the rain and the wind persisted.

The prospect of spending more than an hour in the cavern annoyed him. He wanted to reach the lodge as soon as possible, and he was inclined to ride out before the storm ended completely. Such exposure, though, would aggravate Sitting Bear's condition, and he resigned himself to staying put for the time being.

With nothing better to do, Nate ruminated on his future. In a couple of weeks Shakespeare would help him set out beaver traps and teach him the tricks of the trade. The idea of becoming a full-fledged trapper, of relying on his wits and strength to provide his livelihood, appealed to him. He'd learned how to be largely independent since leaving civilization, and the more he learned the better he felt. No longer did he depend on the market and the mercantile for everything under the sun. He could feed and clothe himself. He was his own man, and the feeling of self-reliance was the greatest he'd ever known.

Nate felt sorry for all the people back East who had no idea what they were missing. They went about their humdrum lives, day in and day out, totally reliant on others for their well-being. He would never allow himself to slip into such a deplorable state again, not even—

A scratching noise from the right interrupted his musing.

Twisting, Nate tensed as he laid eyes on a bulky, squat form moving toward him. He rose, leveling the Hawken, unable to identify the creature until a streak of lightning briefly illuminated his surroundings. With the flaring glow came recognition, and with recognition apprehension. The last thing he wanted to do was tangle with a beast that rivaled the grizzly in ferocity.

Coming toward him was a dreaded wolverine.

Chapter Ten

Roughly bearlike in shape, wolverines were considerably smaller than bruins, with the males reaching four feet in length, standing a foot and a half high at the shoulders, and weighing between 40 and 50 pounds when in their prime. But when compared pound for pound with every other mammal on the continent, wolverines rated as the most powerful in existence.

Nate had heard tales galore about the prowess of the gluttons, as they were commonly called. Wolverines had been known to drive panthers and grizzlies from their kills, and one trapper had observed a wolverine bring down a full-grown moose trapped in heavy snow. They were notorious for following trap lines and either eating the bait or consuming the animals that had been caught. They also raided cabins, and in the process they would deposit their musk on everything they didn't eat.

The indistinct form flowed nearer, then halted and loudly sniffed the air.

Of all the luck! Nate thought, and cocked the rifle. He didn't know if the creature was entering or leaving the cavern. All he cared about was that it departed, and did so promptly. If the horses got its scent, there would be hell to pay.

Still sniffing, the wolverine took a few steps. Another lightning strike revealed its beady eyes were fixed on Sitting Bear.

Nate deduced the beast must smell the dried blood on the Crow's leggings. Knowing its appetite for any and all flesh, he feared he would have to fight it off. Once the shimmering glare from the heavenly bolt faded, all he could see was the carnivore's black form. If he had to fire in the dark, he couldn't guarantee he would hit it.

The wolverine suddenly growled.

"Go away!" Nate shouted in the hope the sound of his voice would drive the thing off.

Instead, the wolverine moved closer still.

"Go!" Nate bellowed.

Snarling deep in its throat, the beast charged.

Instantly Nate squeezed the trigger. He saw the wolverine jerk backwards and fall, and he thought for a second that he'd killed it. His mistake became apparent the next moment when the animal scrambled to its feet and attacked once more.

This time it bounded toward him.

One of the horses whinnied in terror as Nate drew his right pistol and extended his arm. He stood his ground, his lips compressed, until the wolverine was almost upon him, and then fired the flinklock at close range.

Again the animal was hit, and again it spun around and went down. As before, it heaved erect and leaped.

There was no opportunity to reload. Nate

released the pistol, seized the rifle by the barrel, and waited until the wolverine was almost at his very feet before he swung the Hawken like a club. The shock crashed into its skull, dazing it for a moment, and he grabbed at his left pistol to finish the animal off.

Yet another thunderbolt cast the cavern in a bright halo.

Nate could see the wolverine's upturned, feral visage, see its mouth wide and its tapered teeth poised to snap. Startled, he pointed the flintlock at its sloping brow and squeezed the trigger, the booming retort making his ears ring even more.

The ball penetrated the wolverine's head between its eyes, and the brute immediately went into convulsions. It thrashed about on the floor, pawing at the ground as its tail whipped in a circular motion.

Prepared to sell his life dearly should the beast renew its attack, Nate braced himself and raised the Hawken on high. He'd club it with his dying breath, if need be.

The terror of the woods uttered a short hiss, sprawled onto its stomach, and went limp.

Nate remained motionless for a full minute before he dared poke the creature with the rifle. After prodding it four times he smiled and vented a sigh of heartfelt relief. Another few inches and the wolverine would have had him.

Outside, the rain and the wind slackened, the downpour becoming a drizzle. Most of the lightning and thunder now occurred to the east.

The horses were fidgeting, so Nate went over and calmed them before attending to the reloading of his guns. He stepped to the cavern mouth and watched the storm clouds sailing rapidly in the direction of the lodge. To the west sunshine caused the soaked vegetation to glisten.

Eager to get going, Nate nevertheless delayed mounting until the rain completely stopped. When he headed out, he stuck to the clearer tracts between the trees to avoid brushing against the drenched limbs and being drenched to his skin. He looked back at the cavern only once, wondering if he should have skinned the wolverine, and decided it was too late to turn around.

The pristine forest seemed renewed by the rain, washed clean of all dirt and dust. Even the wildlife was invigorated. The birds came to life with renewed vitality, warbling or chirping songs in joyous abandon.

Mankind could learn a lot from Nature, Nate reflected. Animals knew how to live life to its fullest; they displayed a passionate zest for existence that most humans sorely lacked. Where men and women were prone to gripe about their lives and bemoan their fates, the animals simply accepted their place in the scheme of things and savored every moment.

Nate pushed the stallion faster than before. He was worried that Sitting Bear had not regained consciousness, and speculated the Crow's life would depend on Evening Star's ministrations. So it was that he smiled broadly when he glimpsed the meandering stream through the trees and shortly thereafter emerged from the woods. He glanced to the right and left, and off to the north stood the lodge, maybe a quarter of a mile distant. At last!

Bringing the stallion to a gallop, Nate covered the wet ground swiftly. Farther to the east was the storm. Thanks to the heavy downpour, the stream had expanded a foot on either side, the water rushing at twice its previous rate. He noticed a log floating downstream. Calmly perched on top, apparently enjoying the ride, was a chipmunk.

Nate expected to see the mother or the boys in the vicinity of the lodge, but none of them were in evidence. He also observed there was no smoke curling up from the top, which he deemed odd since the temperature had dropped a few degrees. Perhaps, he reasoned, they'd taken shelter inside when the storm approached and simply stayed there.

Unexpectedly, Sitting Bear mumbled a few words and stirred. His head snapped up and he looked around.

"It's all right," Nate said, unable to use sign language. "We'll be with your family in a bit."

The Crow spoke a single word, then sagged.

As yet no one had appeared.

"Evening Star! Strong Wolf!" Nate shouted. "Get out here!" He focused on the flap, anticipating it would open, and when he covered another 40 yards without anyone coming out he reined up, certain something was wrong. Even though the family couldn't speak English, they knew his voice. At the very least one of the boys would venture from the lodge to investigate.

Sitting Bear began muttering.

Nate scanned the woods and the field. Sparrows flitted about in the trees immediately behind the lodge, which indicated there was no one lurking in the forest. He looked at the field on the other side of the stream again, and realized with a start that his mare and pack animal were gone.

Stunned, Nate rode to the lodge and halted ten feet from the door. Only then did he see the slash marks in the buffalo skin and a broken bow lying in the dirt nearby. He quickly dismounted and lowered the Crow to the ground, then hefted the Hawken and advanced to the flap.

Something moved to his left.

Nate spun, his thumb on the hammer, and was horrified to see Strong Wolf crawling from the high weeds. The boy's face and shoulders were caked with blood. "No!" he cried, and ran to the youth, stopping a foot short when he laid eyes on top of the boy's head and discovered someone had scalped him. "No," he repeated weakly.

Strong Wolf had his neck craned so he could look up, an eloquent appeal mirrored in his eyes. He said a sentence in Crow, the words rasping in his throat, and coughed up crimson spittle.

Kneeling, Nate placed his hand on the youth's right shoulder. He saw a wide trail of blood extending back into the weeds and shuddered.

Gritting his teeth, Strong Wolf raised his right arm and pointed at the lodge.

Nate nodded and sprinted to the doorway. He opened the flap and ducked inside, the Hawken at the ready, prepared for anything. Or so he believed until he beheld the savagely butchered form of Red Hawk in the middle of the floor. The boy's hands had been hacked off and his eyes gouged out. His mouth hung wide, exposing the fact his tongue was gone. Nausea swamped Nate, forcing him to back from the lodge and gasp for fresh air. No matter how many times he witnessed the results of the atrocities Indians perpetrated against one another, he couldn't get used to such merciless slaughter.

A questioning voice diverted his morbid thoughts.

Nate swung around to find Sitting Bear trying

to sit and gazing about in bewildered anxiety. He walked to the warrior and signed for him to lay back down.

The Crow did so, then lifted his head. "Where is my family?"

"I do not know yet," Nate partly lied.

"They should be here."

"Rest. I will check on them."

"I should help," Sitting Bear said, pressing his palms on the grass.

"No," Nate responded. "You are in no condition to get up. Stay where you are and I will take care of everything."

Reluctantly, the Crow complied. His eyes closed and he breathed noisily.

Swiftly Nate returned to Stong Wolf, who had collapsed onto his forearms, and squatted.

The boy glanced at him and feebly manipulated his hands. "Is my brother dead?"

"Yes," Nate answered, sadness filling his soul.

"My mother and sister?"

"They were not in the teepee."

Strong Wolf gazed at his father. "What happened?"

"The Utes attacked us," Nate explained, eager to pose queries of his own. "What happened here?"

"More Utes," Strong Wolf responded, moving his arms with considerable effort.

"Let me roll you over," Nate proposed.

"No."

"You will be able to use your hands easier," Nate explained, and gingerly grasped the boy by the shoulders. Despite a frantic shake of Strong Wolf's head, he rolled the youth onto his back. And promptly wished he hadn't.

The young Crow had been gutted, his abdomen

sliced open from side to side, and his intestines dangled from the cavity.

Nate recoiled, aghast.

"I tried to spare you," Strong Wolf said, his hands gesturing sluggishly.

A sudden, red-hot rage made Nate tingle. He gazed into the boy's eyes and saw reflected a knowledge of the inevitable. Still, he had to try. "Do not move. I will make bandages."

"You would be wasting your time. I am dead."

Nate could only swallow. Hard.

"Will my father live?"

"I honestly cannot say."

Profound sorrow lined the youth's tender visage. "The Utes will have much to celebrate."

"Tell me what happened," Nate prompted.

Strong Wolf licked his lips and inhaled deeply. "They came just before the rain, a band of nine warriors. Red Hawk and I were practicing with our bows and saw the war party riding toward us from the southwest. I knew we could not protect our mother and sister from so many, so I sent him into the lodge to get them while I ran to your horses." He paused. "We would have returned them."

A peculiar lump had formed in Nate's throat.

"The Utes were faster than I thought, and they were on us before I could bring the horses. I saw Red Hawk push Mother and Laughing Eyes inside while he blocked the doorway and defended them. And then six of them attacked me. I put an arrow in one," Strong Wolf related proudly.

"Did you see what happened to your mother and sister?"

"No. I heard them screaming and the laughter of the Utes, who had left me for dead in the field after scalping me." Strong Wolf blinked, and there were tears in his eyes. "I wanted to help them, but could not."

"You did all any man could have done."

"I am not yet a man."

"You are in my eyes."

A smile creased the youth's lips. He abruptly arched his back, uttered a strangled whine, and died, his wide eyes fixed on the bright blue sky.

For a minute Nate didn't budge, too overcome with emotion. His mind seemed to be swirling like a tornado, and there was a bitter taste in his mouth. These had been decent, friendly people, people he'd grown to like, people he was proud to know. To have their lives so callously taken was the height of injustice. The boys' best years had been ahead of them, and now they were nothing more than mutilated corpses awaiting the embrace of the cold earth.

He stared into the distance, a fiery resolve solidifying within him, a grim determination to see those responsible punished. If he didn't seek retribution, no one else would. If nothing else, he could attempt to rescue Evening Star and Laughing Eyes and see them and Sitting Bear safely to their tribe.

Nate stood, his mind made up. One way or the other, the Utes were going to pay. Even if it cost him his own life.

Chapter Eleven

Nate was seated next to the fire, dozing off about midnight, when a firm hand nudged his left leg. He snapped awake, staring blankly at the interior of the lodge until gruesome memories of the events of the day returned in a rush.

Again someone nudged him.

Fully alert, Nate glanced down at the Crow warrior lying on his left. He smiled and used his hands to say, "How are you feeling?"

"A little better," Sitting Bear signed, and looked around. "Where is my family?"

Nate hesitated.

"Tell the truth," the warrior admonished.

Although loath to add to the man's misery, Nate complied. "Strong Wolf and Red Hawk are dead, killed by Utes."

"And my wife and daughter?"

"I wish I knew. I could not find their bodies, so I believe the Utes took them."

Sitting Bear closed his eyes and sighed.

Had he fallen asleep again? Nate wondered

hopefully.

The Crow looked up again, profound inner pain lining his countenance. "This has been the saddest day of my life. I have lost the boys who were the joy of my heart, and because of my wound I cannot go after the fish-eaters who have taken the rest of my family. What have I done to deserve such anguish?"

"You did nothing."

"I must have done something. All suffering is for a purpose."

Nate studied the warrior's face, amazed the man could be so calm after learning of the death of his sons. Or was Sitting Bear crying inside, where it hurt the most? "I will make you some stew to eat," he offered.

"There is another thing you must do."

"What?"

"Save Evening Star and Laughing Eyes. The Utes will take them to their village. You must intercept the band before then or my wife and daughter will be lost forever."

"I plan to go after them as soon as you recover enough to take care of yourself."

"Go now."

"I cannot."

"Why not?"

"Even if I wanted to, it would do no good. I cannot track at night."

Sitting Bear peered at the top of the lodge. "Stars. I did not notice them before." He stared at Nate. "Then you must go at first light."

"I will not leave you alone."

"Then take me with you."

"You must be delirious. You know you are in no condition to travel."

Exasperation flicked across the warrior's face.

"Surely you understand that my life is unimportant. You must save my wife and daughter and not worry about me. Leave enough jerked meat for me to get by and some water. I will be fine."

Nate frowned. "I am sorry. No."

Sitting Bear put his hands on the floor and endeavored to sit, but he only succeeded in rising to his elbows. He swayed, then sank down with a groan.

"See? You are too weak to fend for yourself. If I left you behind, it would be the same as killing you," Nate told him.

"Please go after them in the morning."

"No."

"I beg you."

"No," Nate signed emphatically. "Now rest while I prepare food."

The Crow's mouth compressed into a thin line.

Feeling supremely guilty, Nate devoted his attention to cooking a tasty bowl of stew using the remains of a rabbit he'd shot earlier for his own supper. Both the buffalo and buck meat had been stolen by the Utes.

As he heated the water he noticed a smudge of dirt on the back of his left hand, reminding him of the hour he'd spent digging graves and burying the two boys, and thinking about the grisly job turned his stomach. He remembered how full of vitality they had been, and he could well imagine the depth of Sitting Bear's love for them.

The warrior grunted.

Nate turned to discover the Crow sitting up, flushed from the effort. "You should not exert yourself," he advised.

"I must convince you I am well enough to take care of myself," Sitting Bear replied. "If not, I must take more drastic steps."

"What do you mean?"

Ignoring the question, the warrior examined the charred hole in his side. "Did you do this?"

"Yes. It was the only way I could think of to stop the bleeding."

"You did well." Sitting Bear gazed at the wall. "Those vermin even took our parfleches. All my wife's herbs were in one of them."

"I can collect more herbs tomorrow if you will describe the plants to me," Nate said.

"You will not be here tomorrow," Sitting Bear stubbornly insisted. "Not if you are truly my friend. I would do the same for you if the situation were reversed."

"I will think about it," Nate offered in the hope of having the subject changed.

The warrior smiled wanly. "Once you have done so, you will realize you must go after them."

Nate placed a few extra limbs on the fire to build up the flames. He gathered an armful of wood before settling down for the night, and he hoped it would be enough to last them until dawn.

"You must be very careful tracking the Utes," Sitting Bear mentioned, apparently taking Nate's departure for granted. "They are extremely clever. My people have fought them for many generations, yet we have not wiped them out yet."

"I do not intend to get my head shot off."

"The war party probably headed southeast toward their main hunting grounds. All Ute villages are in that direction. The nearest will be two or three days off. You must ride hard to overtake them," the Crow said. "Is your mare a good animal?"

"They stole my mare and pack animal."

Sitting Bear's mouth dropped. "Then how will you ever catch them?"

"We brought back the three horses belonging to the warriors who attacked us, remember?"

"No."

"You revived somewhat when we were riding back. I thought you would," Nate said. "One of the animals is a fine black stallion. I will use it."

"They will stay close to the stream for the first day, then take a trail that leads to the Green River."

Nate stirred the stew and tasted its temperature with his right index finger, then turned to the Crow. "There is something I do not understand."

"What?"

"I suspect the three Utes we fought were the ones who tried to sneak up on us last night. But where did the second group come from? And why did the larger party attack your family instead of us? If all of them had gone after us, we would never have stood a chance."

Sitting Bear suddenly pressed his hand to his temple. He swayed for a moment and sat down.

"Are you all right?"

"A little dizzy. It will pass," the warrior said. "As for your question, the four who crept up on the lodge must have been part of the larger war party. When you drove them off, they went back to their companions and told them what had happened. Then they watched our camp and saw us leave."

"We should never have gone."

The comment made Sitting Bear's face become a mask of sorrow. "I agree. The blame is all mine."

Nate realized his mistake and promptly urged, "Go on with what you were saying."

"In order for the warriors who were driven off to prove their courage, they came after us themselves. I wish all of them had done so."

Nate swept the lodge with his gaze. "Why did they leave your teepee standing?"

A faint hint of a smile curled Sitting Bear's mouth. "Indians rarely steal lodges. It is difficult for a war party to make an effective escape while dragging twelve or more poles the size of small trees and a heavy buffalo-hide cover."

Amazed that the man could joke in the midst of such tragedy, Nate grinned and tested the stew again. It still wasn't hot enough. He moved closer to the warrior. "Let me feel your forehead."

"Why?"

"To see if you have a fever."

"I am fine."

"I want to see for myself," Nate stressed, and placed his left palm above Sitting Bear's brow. For an instant he had the impression he'd touched a scorching coal. "You are burning up."

"I may have a slight fever," the Crow allowed.

"You must lie down and rest. If you overexert yourself, there could be serious complications. Trust me."

"Are you a healer?"

"No, but I know a little about medicine."

"White man's medicine."

"And what is wrong with our medicine?"

"I do not know exactly because I have never met a white medicine man, although I was told such do exist. But they must not be very skilled because whites are so unhealthy."

"We are not," Nate said.

"Then why is it so many white men get mouth

rot? My people never have problems with their teeth, yet in white men such a disgusting condition is quite common."

Nate had no answer for that one. Shakespeare had told him that tooth decay was unknown among the tribes.

"And if your medicine men do know what they are doing, then why do quite a number of white men suffer from a whirling brain?" Sitting Bear went on.

"I do not know," Nate admitted. When an Indian said someone's brain was in a whirl, it meant the person was insane.

"Our medicine men teach us valuable things like which foods are best and those we should avoid. They keep us healthy at all times, and that is why we live so much longer than you whites. In my village alone there are eleven men who have seen over one hundred winters go by, yet I have never heard of a white living that long."

"Few of us do."

Sitting Bear nodded. "Beause your medicine is wrong or weak or both. Perhaps your Great Chief should send white medicine men to us and we will train them properly."

"I will mention your idea to the Great Chief the next time I am in . . ." Nate paused because there was no hand gesture for Washington, D.C. He finished the statement using language the Crow would understand. " . . . the village where all our chiefs gather."

"Does this village have a name?"

"Yes, but it is unlike any name you know."

"Tell me."

Nate did so, employing English.

Clearly perplexed, Sitting Bear repeated it several times. "You are right. I have never heard such a strange name. What does it mean?"

"The city was named after our first Great Chief, the man who defeated the British and secured peace for us all."

Sitting Bear nodded. "You refer to the war between the redcoats and the tea-drinkers. Yes, I known all about it from a trapper." He stopped and pondered for a moment. "Is it true what he told me about the manner of fighting in that war?"

"What did he say?"

"That when both sides wanted to fight, they would march up to each other in straight rows, stop, and shoot until one side or the other had lost too many men to continue."

Nate grinned. "Some of the battles were fought in that way, yes."

"And they did not hide behind trees or rocks?"

"Not in those instances."

Sitting Bear shook his head slowly. "White men are so strange. I do not understand why the Great Mystery put them in this world."

"Some white men have wondered the same thing."

The warrior looked into Nate's eyes. "Please do not be offended by my remarks. They do not apply to you. Out of all the men I have known, you are one of the bravest. And in your inner spirit you are very much an Indian."

"Thank you," Nate responded, feeling self-conscious at being the subject of such blatant flattery.

"I mean every word, Grizzly Killer. You are a man who is at home in the wilderness. You will never leave it."

The assertion troubled Nate. He thought of his parents and friends and Adeline. Especially Adeline. "One day I might, just to visit those I love."

"But you will be back."

"How can you be so sure?"

"It is your nature," Sitting Bear signed.

Nate heard the stew boiling and turned to it. The tantalizing aroma of the rabbit filled the lodge. He stirred the stew, thinking about New York City. Maybe he wouldn't go back after all. The prospect of being away from Winona for a month or two was singularly unappealing. Perhaps it would be for the best if his family never heard from him again. They'd simply assume he'd been slain and go on with their lives after a period of mourning. Why stir them up by going back?

Some things were better left alone.

Chapter Twelve

Nate awakened to the cheerful sounds of chirping birds. He rolled onto his back, stretched, and sat up. Sunlight streamed in the open doorway, which puzzled him because he knew he'd shut the flap before retiring. He idly glanced at the fire and received a shock.

Sitting Bear was already awake and in the process of preparing the morning meal. He wore a clean pair of leggings and had washed the dried blood from his body. Arranged in his hair were the five eagle feathers obtained at such a terrible price. He looked around and smiled. "Time to greet the new day."

"What are you doing up?" Nate asked while sliding out from under his blanket.

"One of us had to make breakfast and you were sound asleep."

"That is not what I meant. You should be resting, taking it easy until your wound heals." Nate stood.

"I wanted to prove to you that I am capable of

taking care of myself so you will go after my wife and daughter," the warrior explained. "I have prepared a pouch containing lots of berries and wild onions. I also saddled the black stallion for you."

Nate glanced at the door. "Saddled him?"

"Yes. I found your saddle in the field where the Utes must have tossed it. They are not very fond of the kind white men use."

A rejoinder concerning Indian saddles was on the tip of Nate's tongue, but he kept his peace. Many Indians liked the simplicity of bareback riding, but there were those who used saddles that were constructed from rawhide and stuffed with grass or buffalo hair. While the Indians considered them comfortable, the whites genereally disdained them.

"So will you save Evening Star and Laughing Eyes?" Sitting Bear inquired anxiously.

Nate bent over to retrieve his rifle, giving himself time to weigh all the factors involved. His friend was mending much faster than he'd anticipated, and it certainly seemed as if Sitting Bear would fare all right on his own. There was also the fact that the sooner he started, the sooner he'd be reunited with Winona. Straightening, Nate nodded, tucked the Hawken under his arm, and used sign to say, "I will leave right away."

Raw relief was mirrored on the Crow's countenance. "You have made me the happiest man alive. But first you should eat. You will need all your strength to kill the fish-eaters."

Nate attended to his morning toilet, ate, and went out again to mount the stallion. Once in the saddle he glanced at the spot where he'd buried the butchered boys, keenly aware the same fate awaited him if he failed, then wheeled the horse. He looked at the doorway and saw Sitting Bear watching him.

"May the Great Mystery guide your footsteps."

Nate nodded and rode to the southeast, feeling the warm sun of his cheeks and a light breeze in his hair. The stream was at its former level, enabling him to cross easily, and soon he had settled into the flowing rhythm of the stallion. Thankfully, the horse didn't mind the saddle, leading him to surmise a previous owner had used an Indian version.

True to Sitting Bear's prediction, Nate found plenty of fresh tracks to indicate the war party had indeed healed the same way. Since the Utes had evidently ridden off just as the storm passed on, the prints of their animals were distinctly imbedded in the soil. He had no difficulty following them.

He worried about how he would save the mother and daughter once he caught up with the band. Nine Utes were formidable opposition. He'd have to improvise, to use his head. Above all, he had to ensure he spotted them before they saw him. The element of surprise was in his favor, the only advantage he possessed, and without it rescuing the Crows was a forlorn proposition.

The minutes went by swiftly, as did the terrain. Nate pushed the stallion, hoping to catch up with the war party before nightfall, encountering abundant wildlife everywhere. There were herds of elk and buffalo, squirrels chittering in the trees, ravens soaring on the air currents, and an occasional predator or two in the form of a wolf or a fox. As always, he felt as if he were traveling through a veritable paradise, a Garden of Eden where many of the animals simply stood and stared at him because they had not yet learned to fear the mere sight of a human being as did their bestial cousins back East.

He stopped at midday and rested on the bank of the stream while munching on a wild onion. Minnows darted about in the water, and an insect that resembled a thin spider swam from side to side on the surface. After consuming the snack he knelt and drank deeply, savoring the cold liquid.

Once in the saddle, Nate resumed his south-easterly journey. He estimated the Utes were no more than two or three hours ahead and moving much slower than he was. Apparently they believed themselves safe from reprisals. He was a bit surprised they hadn't waited for their three companions to catch up. But then, maybe the reason they were going so slowly was to give the trio an opportunity to do just that. Little did they know the threesome would never lift another scalp.

At one point he spied an enormous grizzly bear off to the east. The monster watched him go by, its kingly composure undisturbed, and did not display any aggression.

The stream wound through a series of low hills, then flowed into a wide valley. Antelope and deer filled their bellies on high grass. Ground squirrels scampered from his path. It took him an hour to traverse the valley. Beyond, the tracks took a course between two hills, and there lay a small plain hemmed by mountains. He reined up in surprise when he saw a column of smoke curling skyward on the far side.

Puzzled, Nate angled toward a stand of trees a few hundred yards to the right. The Utes must have stopped, but he couldn't understand why. Plenty of daylight remained, and it seemed unlikely the Indians would waste it without a good reason. He studied the position of the smoke and deduced the camp was almost three quarters of a mile away.

Off to the south five vultures circled high above the landscape, seeking carrion.

Nate rode into the trees, a cluster of cottonwoods, and dismounted. He secured the reins to a limb and ventured to the south edge where he could see the smoke unobstructed. Now what should he do? Trying to approach the camp when the sun was up qualified as certain suicide. The wise thing to do was wait until nightfall.

The whinny of a horse came from the north.

Startled, Nate pivoted and beheld a pair of Indians heading in the direction of the smoke. They were less than 50 yards off, both mounted and both armed with bows.

Utes!

Nate crouched and slid behind the trunk of a cottonwood. One of the Indian mounts whinnied again. He wondered if the animal had detected the airborne scent of the stallion, and he moved toward his horse to prevent it from answering. But he was too late.

The black stallion vented a neigh loud enough to rouse a hibernating bear.

Halting in midstride, Nate saw the warriors stop and look at the trees. Would they investigate or keep going? He hefted the Hawken and waited for their reaction, barely breathing.

The pair turned their steeds and rode straight toward the cottonwoods.

Nate hurried to the stallion, keeping as low as he could and using the boles for cover. He didn't want to tangle with the duo if a conflict could be avoided. Gunshots were bound to alert the rest of the Utes.

Fidgeting and tugging on the reins, the stallion had its eyes on the approaching horses.

Quickly Nate reached his animal and wrapped his left arm around its muzzle. He could see the Indians through the trees. Neither betrayed any hint of alarm. They appeared to be mainly curious. He began to guide the stallion to the west, moving slowly, hoping the shadows screened them from hostile eyes.

The taller of the warriors halted and made a motion as if he wanted to continue on to their camp. Responding in the Ute tongue, the second man kept coming.

Nate stopped within a yard from the last of the cottonwoods. He held the stallion still except for the twitching of its tail, and rubbed its neck to keep it calm.

The inquisitive Ute reined up near the trees and peered into the stand, leaning forward, his dark eyes narrowed. He scanned from right to left and back again.

This was the moment of truth, Nate realized. The stand was approximately 30 yards in diameter, and many of the cottonwoods were quite large. Plenty of underbrush further served to counceal him and his mount. The odds of escaping detection were excellent provided the stallion cooperated.

Evidently satisfied there was nothing to see, the Ute turned his steed.

Suddenly the big horse acted up, trying to pull from Nate's grasp. Its buttocks bumped a trunk.

Nate held on with all of his might. He saw the Ute twist and look back, and he was certain the

warrior would ride into the stand to check things
out. Instead, after a minute, the Ute rejoined his
fellow tribesman and together they made to the
southeast.

Relief washed over Nate and he expelled a long
breath. He stayed where he was until the
warriors were far away, then let go of the stallion. That had been too close! He'd have to
be much more careful in the future or Evening
Star and Laughing Eyes would never be rescued.

Deciding to remain in the stand until evening,
Nate moved to the center, tied the stallion so it
wouldn't get any ideas about wondering off, and
sat down with his back to the trunk. He devoted
himself to formulating a strategy for dealing with
the war party. When the time came to snatch the
mother and daughter, a diversion might enable
him to pull it off without a hitch. What kind of
diversion, though? He formulated and discarded
various ideas, absently listening to the sounds of
insects and the songs of the birds. After a while
his eyelids began to droop, and before he knew
it he was asleep.

A sharp noise brought Nate rudely awake, and
he glanced up in consternation when he realized
darkness had descended. How long had he slept?
He stood, amazed to see faint stars through the
branches, and looked westward where hues of
red, orange, and pink rimmed the horizon. The
sun had set within the past half hour, he guessed.

The stallion shifted, one of its hooves cracking
a twig with a pronounced snap.

Now Nate knew what had wakened him. He
undid the reins, climbed on board, and rode out
of the cottonwoods, bearing in the direction of
the Ute encampment. A flickering ghost of light

marked the exact location. He shook his head to clear his mind of lingering sluggishness, and surveyed the plain in case there were warriors ahead.

The war party, as it turned out, had made camp at the base of a densely wooded slope on the east side of the narrow stream. There was plenty of water, plenty of game, and the forest gave them a convenient avenue of retreat should they be attacked by a superior force.

Nate perceived there were actually two fires, not one, spaced ten yards apart, and he distinguished figures moving around the camp. He slanted to the right, riding toward the woods bordering the plain. The same forest that the Utes would use as an avenue of escape was also their weak spot. Moving slowly as not to create enough noise to give himself away, he gained the cover of the woods without mishap. The steadily gathering gloom compelled him to cautiously pick his way among the trees until he reached the slope to the rear of the band. After tying the stallion yet again at a sufficient distance from the enemy to ensure they couldn't hear it should the horse neigh, he crept through the vegetation toward the fires.

Laughter and boisterous conversation arose, contrasting with the deathly stillness of the forest. Nate bent over at the waist as he covered the final 20 yards, advancing from trunk to trunk and thicket to thicket. Less than eight feet from the end of the woods he flattened and crawled to a cluster of high weeds at the very limit. Inching his right hand foward, he gingerly parted the stalks and leaves.

Both fires were only 25 feet off. To the right were the tethered horses, including the mare and the pack animal. Five Utes were seated around the fire on the left. Four warriors were sitting near the one opposite. Laughing Eyes sat on the ground close to them, watching her mother serve food to the band.

Nate congratulated himself on his cleverness. Perhaps a diversion wouldn't be needed, after all. If he waited long enough, the Utes were bound to go to sleep. He learned from Shakespeare that Indians rarely posted guards at night unless they were certain of being attacked.

A strapping warrior unexpectedly stood and walked directly toward him.

Chapter Thirteen

Nate froze, not knowing what to do, afraid to so much as blink. Panic seized him, and for a moment he believed the Ute must have spotted him. Only when he observed the warrior hitch at the leggings he wore did comprehension dawn. He relaxed slightly, his left hand holding the rifle firmly.

Whistling softly, the Ute glanced over his shoulder and made a comment that caused the others to laugh. He paused, studying the trees, and finally stepped to the right and disappeared behind a towering pine.

Straining his ears, Nate detected the splattering of urine on the ground. He dared not turn his head, and didn't until the warrior emerged and moved back to the campfire.

Another Ute barked a command at Evening Star, who promptly went over to him.

Nate saw one of the warriors wearing a crude rawhide bandage, and realized it must be the Indian Strong Wolf had wounded. The man was in a bad way, doubled over and holding his left side, sitting almost on top of the flames. A chest wound, Nate guessed, and probably close to the heart.

Evening Star was busily cutting meat from a cooked haunch, her despondent features reflecting the misery in her soul.

From the aroma Nate's nostrils detected, he knew the band was eating part of the buffalo he'd slain, and he wryly wished the meat would give them all indigestion. A lean Ute sporting four eagle feathers in his hair rose and went to the horses, returning moments later bearing a parfleche stolen from Sitting Bear's lodge. Nate recognized it as the one in which Evening Star stored her herbs and medicines from the decorative beadwork on the pouch.

The lean warrior knelt alongside his wounded fellow, then snapped a sentence at the Crow woman.

Obediently, Evening Star ceased working on the meat and hurried off. The parfleche was shoved into her hands, and a curt gesture from the Ute signified she should tend to the one who had been shot.

Nate scowled in anger. The war party was using her to do every chore imaginable, reducing her to the status of a slave. He thought about the nine or ten hours of night remaining and his scowl deepened. Would they abuse her in *that* manner too?

Evening Star opened her bag and took out some herbs. Next she removed the injured warrior's bandages, then proceeded to administer treatment.

A deep admiration for her courage caused Nate to think of his own wife, who had demonstrated her own resourcefulness more than once. He unconsciously compared them to Adeline Van Buren, imagining how the socialite would behave under the same circumstances, and almost laughed aloud. Adeline would have been in hysterics by now, pleading with her captors to let her go and offering them all the wealth her father owned.

Nate rested his chin on his forearms and bided his time. The Utes talked and talked. After nursing the wounded warrior and feeding the others, Evening Star was permitted to take her daughter in her arms and sit off a ways. Four of the Utes retired relatively early, curling up in their robes and falling asleep.

A northwesterly breeze kicked up, fanning the flames and carrying glowing red sparks aloft.

The hours dragged by. Nate was impatient for the remainder to doze off, and finally all did but two. This pair was engaged in an earnest dialogue and gave no indication of stopping soon. Evening Star had been given a blanket, and she was lying on her back with Laughing Eyes at her side.

To the west a wolf howled.

Nate speculated the time must be after midnight, and he wondered if the talkative twosome intended to stay awake all night. He felt stiff from lying on the ground for so long, and he keenly desired to stretch his legs.

A minute later the last of the war party lay down to sleep.

Nervous expectation revitalized Nate. He waited a reasonable length of time to guarantee the Utes were all slumbering, then eased backwards, twisted, and crawled to the right, keeping to the edge of the woods until he was directly to the rear of the horses. Now came the perilous part. His gaze riveted on the Utes, he inched from the vegetation and slid to the animals, expecting at any second that one of the war party would awaken, spot him, and shriek a warning to the others.

A few of the horses heard him and glanced back, but none snorted or reared.

Nate reached the mare and slowly rose, his knees bent, stooped over, and stepped to her neck. He rubbed her behind the ears and whispered softly, letting her know there was no reason to be skittish. The Utes had tied all of the animals to a pair of logs, evidently hauled from the forest for that very purpose, to guarantee the horses wouldn't stray away during the night. He moved to the log and quickly untied the mare, then did the same with his pack animal. Gripping the reins of both, he led them into the trees at a snail's pace, and when he had put a good 15 yards behind them he went faster, taking the two horses to where he'd left the stallion. He secured both and hastened back.

The Utes were still sleeping soundly.

Exercising the same care as before, Nate crawled to the horses again. Earlier he'd seen a rope lying next to one of the logs, and he now used it to prepare a little surprise for the Indians. Going from horse to horse, he looped the rope around the front legs of each animal, then securely knotted the end to the log. That done, he crept to the Crows.

Mother and daughter were sound asleep. In the flickering light from the fading fire tear streaks were visible on Evening Star's cheeks. She had her left arm draped protectively over Laughing Eyes.

Nate crouched, then hesitated. All around were sleeping Utes, and any loud noise would bring them to their feet in a rush. He gently placed his right hand on the mother's shoulder and squeezed.

Evening Star's eyes snapped open and she looked up. Astonishment caused her to gape until she had recovered sufficiently to smile broadly.

Nate pressed a finger to his lips, and was gratified when she nodded to indicate her understanding. He held the Hawken in both hands and covered the band while Evening Star lifted her daughter.

A nearby Ute tossed in his sleep and mumbled for a bit.

Motioning for the mother to precede him, Nate gestured at the trees and waited until she went ten feet before he followed. The rescue had turned out to be much easier than he'd anticipated, and he wondered if the Utes didn't have an unjustified reputation as fierce fighters.

At that instant, with Evening Star just reaching the shelter of the woods, a muscular warrior lying close to the nearest fire abruptly sat up and gazed about him in drowsy curiosity, as if he wasn't quite sure why he had woken up. His gaze alighted on Nate and he blinked in disbelief.

Backpedaling, Nate trained the rifle on the Ute and cocked the hammer. He still had a few feet to go to the forest when the Indian leapt erect, whipped out a knife, and vented a strident whoop. Nate shot him.

The rest of the war party awakened immediately, the warriors scrambling to their feet and voicing bewildered exclamations.

Spinning, Nate took a bound and plunged into the woods. Evening Star was waiting for him, and he grasped her elbow and propelled her in the direction of the horses.

Shouts and bellows of rage arose in the encampment.

Nate repeatedly looked back as he ran, searching for the telltale silhouettes of pursuers, certain the band would be after them any second.

In confirmation, four warriors materialized at the edge of the woods, their forms backlit by the firelight. They peered into the murky woods, and one of them called out and pointed. All four leaped forward.

Nate prodded Evening Star. She understood and pumped her legs harder, clasping Laughing Eyes to her bosom, tearing loose from occasional limbs that snatched at her buckskin dress.

The Utes voiced shrill shrieks, a veritable pack of frenzied wolves closing in for the kill.

Keeping pace with the Crow woman, Nate marveled at her fleetness. She ran like a terrified doe, leaping logs and adroitly skirting trunks and dense bushes. He glimpsed Laughing Eyes awake and staring at him, her eyes wide. Incredibly, the girl didn't cry or scream.

A minute went by.

The vague shapes of the horses appeared in the darkness.

Nate glanced back, thinking they would get away without further incident, and discovered that one of the Utes had outstripped his companions and was now less than 15 feet off. The warrior held a tomahawk in his right hand.

Nate had a choice to make. Either he confronted the Ute now and gave the Crows time to reach the horses, or he waited until they were at the animals and exposed mother and daughter to the wrath of the warrior. There really wasn't a choice at all. He halted and whirled, drawing the right flintlock.

Roaring in triumph, the Ute raised the tomahawk overhead and came straight at him.

In a flash Nate extended his arm and squeezed off a shot. The ball hit the Indian squarely in the center of his chest, and he flipped backwards and sprawled in the weeds. Not bothering to verify the kill, Nate turned, and was surprised to find Evening Star had stopped to wait for him. "Go!" he urged, well aware she couldn't understand him.

Now that he was safe, the woman resumed her flight and came to the horses. She paused and looked at Nate, apparently awaiting instructions.

Nate indicated the mare, awkwardly took Laughing Eyes into his arms, and waited for Evening Star to mount. He handed the girl up and stepped to the stallion.

Out of nowhere streaked an arrow to thud into a tree a couple of feet away.

Hastily wedging the flintlock under his belt, Nate seized the reins and swung into the saddle. He grabbed the lead for the pack animal, wheeled the big black, and made off to the northwest. Instead of sticking to the forest, he intended to cut directly across the plain. The level ground would be easier to traverse, and the Utes might not perceive the strategy until it was too late.

Yelling erupted to their rear.

Nate led the Crows rapidly through the trees to the grassland and galloped from cover without a second thought. He slanted toward the distant stand of cottonwoods and glanced to the right.

A raucous commotion was taking place in the Ute encampment. Evidently one of the warriors had tried to give chase on a horse and discovered the animals were tied together. Some of the band were staring into the forest and talking excitedly. Not one was paying attention to the plain.

Yet.

Nate kept the stallion next to the mare. He was uncomfortable having only one gun still loaded, and wished to reach the stand quickly so he could attend to the Hawken and the expended pistol. After that, his next priority would be to locate a safe hiding place where they could stay until morning.

Evening Star glanced at him and grinned. She said a single word in Crow.

Although Nate didn't know the term, he intuitively knew she'd thanked him for saving the two of them. He concentrated on the ground ahead, alert for pale dirt mounds that betokened the presence of animals burrows. Many a horse had stumbled in an unseen badger or prairie dog hole and broken its leg, and for such an accident to occur at that moment would have the direst of consequences.

They made good time, and in due course the stand loomed out of the murky night, appearing as a single, gigantic black mass.

Nate slowed and entered the trees, proceeding until he came to a small clearing, where he climbed down.

The Crows were right on his tail. Evening Star reined up, then performed sign language, moving her hands slowly so he could read them without difficulty. "I thank you for saving us from a life of misery."

Nate stepped up to the mare. "We are not safe yet."

"Why do we stop now?"

"I must reload."

Evening Star gazed around at the cottonwoods. "Where is my husband? He should be with you."

"Sitting Bear was wounded by other Utes. He would have come if he could."

"Where is he now?"

"At your lodge. He begged me to leave him and try to save you."

About to motion in response, Evening Star stiffened and cocked her head.

At the same moment Nate heard the sounds too.

The unmistakable drumming of hooves drawing swiftly nearer.

Chapter Fourteen

There was no time to reload. Nate remounted and led the way to the east. He couldn't imagine how the Utes had found them so quickly, but he did know the band would expect him to take a northwesterly direction, the shortest route back. If he swung eastward for a few miles, he would elude them. Hopefully.

The approaching horses drew abreast of the stand, then went past.

Nate could see the Utes, four in all, riding hard toward the gap between the two hills. He realized the war party had no idea where to find them. The quartet were probably going to guard the gap as a preventative measure, nothing more. Stopping, he waited until the Indians were out of sight, then dropped to the ground and loaded first the Hawken, then the pistol.

Distant yells came from the encampment.

Once back in the saddle, Nate continued to the east. He was briefly worried when they emerged from the sanctuary of the trees onto the open plain, where they could easily be spotted, but their ride to the base of a wide mountain was uneventful. He turned to the north, hoping to locate a different gap or pass. In half a mile they found a gorge that cut sharply to the right, and acting on a hunch he entered it.

The walls of the gorge were 40 feet apart, sheer precipices rearing on high. A few dwarf trees were scattered along the gravel bottom and large boulders were everywhere.

Nate prayed he hadn't taken them into a dead end. Ten minutes later, when they came to an incline on the left, he eagerly rode to the top. Before them stretched a seemingly limitless expanse of forest.

Satisfied that they had escaped, Nate decided to stay on the rim until morning. He communicated his desire to Evening Star, and after the horses were secure they found a comfortable spot under a spreading canyon maple. Laughing Eyes sat in her mother's lap, staring at the country below. He shifted to face them. "I am sorry we cannot use a fire."

"I understand," Evening Star assured him.

"We will wait until daylight, then leave."

"You need not stop on our account."

"It is not safe to travel at night, as you well know," Nate noted. "What difference can four or five more hours make?"

"The Utes will not rest until they recapture us."

"I doubt you have anything to worry about. They will not find us now."

Evening Star did not respond.

Nate leaned against the trunk and let the tension drain from his body. All in all, he'd handled himself well. Shakespeare would be proud. His stomach growled, reminding him of the onions and berries in his pouch, and he wondered if the others were hungry. "Would you like something to eat?"

"No. The Utes let us eat earlier."

Nate went to the stallion and retrieved the pouch, then settled down and munched contentedly on the food. The escapade had taught him a valuable lesson in self-reliance. He could, when the necessity arose, hold his own against some of the toughest warriors in the West. Where before his heart pumped faster at the mere mention of the Utes, now he recognized they were no worse than any other tribe. All the Utes had going for them was an unjustified reputation.

Word of mouth, he determined, had a lot to do with the status of individual men or entire tribes. Embellished by drink or imagination, tales concerning the likes of Jim Bridger, Joseph Walker, and Shakespeare McNair tended to give those mountain men an exaggerated aspect, and the same held true for the Utes and the Blackfeet. For years everyone had been saying those two tribes were the terrors of the Rockies, and now the claim was widely accepted as verified fact. Actually, the Utes were no worse than the Bloods and the Piegans, two lesser known tribes who also killed whites on sight.

Nate listened to animal noises carried by the cool wind. Wolves were particularly active at night, and their howls ranged far and wide. Owls hooted regularly. Now and then a panther would scream like a woman being tortured. And ominous, deep growls sounded from somewhere farther up the gorge.

Evening Star was intently studying Nate. The little girl had reclined on her back, her head on her mother's leg.

"Is something wrong?"

"No," Evening Star answered. "But I wonder about something. May I ask you a question?"

"Go ahead."

"Why did you risk your life to save ours? We hardly know you."

"Your family fed me, sheltered me, treated me as a friend. I could not stand by and let you be abducted."

The woman nodded. "You are an honorable man, Grizzly Killer. You will become great if you do not die first."

Nate smiled and took a bite of onion. In her own way, Evening Star was almost as attractive as Winona. Almost, but not quite. She possessed a calm, stately bearing he admired. Like most Indian women, she was earthy and self-disciplined, the exact opposite of her civilized white sisters in the States. What was it about civilization, he mused, that produced men and women who were overly dependent on the society in which they lived? The longer he lived in the wild, the more convinced he became that too much so-called culture tended to breed physical and moral weaklings.

"You must miss your wife," Evening Star signed.

A frown curled Nate's lip. "With all my heart."

"She is very fortunate to have such a brave husband."

"Sitting Bear is also brave. You should have seen him fight the Utes."

"Did he get the feathers he wanted?"

"Yes."

The Crow sighed and gazed at a small pine tree swaying in the wind. "Then the worst is yet to come."

"What do you mean?" Nate inquired.

"Once he heals, he will try to steal enough horses from the Arapahos to make up for those that were stolen. It will be very dangerous, yet he insists on going alone."

"I could go with him."

Evening Star smiled. "Thank you. But we both know he is too proud. He will never permit you to accompany him. This is something he must do by himself." She paused. "If only my sons were alive. He might have consented to take them."

Nate suddenly lost his appetite. "I am extremely sorry about your boys. They were a credit to their parents and would have grown to be mighty warriors."

The quiet night was abruptly shattered by the crack of a gun from the direction of the plain.

"It must be the Utes," Evening Star declared.

"Why would they fire a shot?" Nate remarked.

"It could be a signal."

"Perhaps," Nate conceded. "But I doubt it has anything to do with us. They cannot possibly know where we are."

"Never underestimate them. They are excellent trackers. By daylight they could pick up our trail."

"By daylight we will be on our way to your lodge. They will never catch up."

"You have much confidence for one so young."

Nate chuckled. "I wish I did."

"Never underestimate yourself," Evening Star said, grinning, and looked at him. "There is another question I would like to ask. A trapper once told me incredible stories about white women and I have often wondered if he spoke the truth. You must know their customs well."

"I know a little about women," Nate said, then added a quote from his mentor, Shakespeare.

"Any man who claims he knows all there is to know is a liar."

Evening Star laughed lightly. "Women find men equally as difficult to understand."

"Even Indian women?"

"Did you think we would be different? Women are women." Evening Star began to tenderly stroke her daughter's hair. "This trapper wanted me to believe that many white women do not marry until they are twenty winters or older. Did he tell the truth?"

"Yes. Some white women marry young, but the trend seems to be for them to marry older and older all the time."

Evening Star shook her head in amazement. "But why do they wait so long and waste so many of their best child-bearing years?"

Nate was about to answer that it simply was the fashion, but there wasn't an equivalent sign gesture. Instead, he shrugged.

"Very mystifying," said Evening Star. "Indian women would not think of waiting twenty winters to marry. As soon as a girl becomes a woman, she is eligible for marriage. Most have a husband by the time they are sixteen."

"How does a girl become a woman?" Nate naively asked.

Evening Star reacted as if surprised by the query. "When she bleeds for the first time."

"Bleeds?" Nate repeated, and then comprehended her meaning. Extremely embarrassed, he pretended to be interested in the eastern horizon, and even made a casual, if inane, comment. "The stars are very bright tonight."

"Yes," the Crow woman replied.

"I do not think I have ever seen them this bright."

"You must not look at the night sky very often."

Taking another bite of onion, Nate saw a brilliant, thin streak of light shoot across the heavens from west to east. A meteor always enthralled him. As a child, he'd always wanted to chase one down and find where it crashed. Meteors served as reminders of the vast, unknown realms existing out among the stars. Many an idle hour had been spent dreaming about the other planets in the solar system: Mercury, Venus, Mars, Jupiter, Saturn, and Uranus.

In a way, his early fascination with the heavens had carried over into his adult life. From his childhood fascination with the mysteries of the universe grew his later fascination with the mysteries awaiting anyone who ventured beyond the Mississippi River in the Great American Desert, as the expanse between the Mississippi and the Pacific Ocean was so frequently called. The unknown held an irresistible allure, a siren call that had beckoned him into the winderness.

More brave souls were answering that call every year. The numbers of trappers and traders was growing rapidly. Shakespeare believed that one day there would be as many people in the West as there were in the East, but Nate was skeptical. For one thing, the Plains and the Rockies were inhabited by dozens of Indian tribes who weren't about to pack up and leave just because the white man wanted to move in. If there ever came a time when the whites did want the land for themselves, there would be hell to pay.

Besides, from what he'd seen, there was no reason the whites and the Indians couldn't live together in harmony. There was enough living space for everyone, and there would never be a shortage of game. The immense herds of buffaloes alone fed millions, and there was little chance of the bison ever dying out.

Nate hoped that he'd never see the day when the current way of life came to an end. There were those, like Shakespeare, who maintained it would, who believed that whites were too greedy and too arrogant to leave well enough alone. There were also those who asserted the U.S. had a right to expand westward to the shores of the Pacific, if need be. So far, their voices were in the minority.

He would be the first to admit that times were changing, though. Why, only a few years ago, Colonel John Stevens, a veteran of the Revolution, had constructed a steam wagon on his estate, a contraption powered by steam and capable of carrying passengers. One day, some claimed, steam-powered devices would replace horses.

About the same time, in Quincy, Massachusetts, a man named Bryant had opened an enterprise he called the Granite Railway. It consisted of horse-drawn wagons that hauled heavy loads effortlessly along miles of hardwood tracks. More such railways were expected to spring up in the years ahead.

The world never stood still, Nate reflected. Change seemed to be the natural order of things, which didn't bode well for the Indians or his peace of mind. All he wanted out of life was the opportunity to live it as he saw fit, without interference from anyone else. And in that respect civilization and the wilderness had something in common. There were always those who took delights in oppressing others, whether it be a tyrannical employer in New York City, or murderous Utes in the Rockies.

Nate glanced at Evening Star and saw she was lying on her back, Laughing Eyes beside her, asleep. He closed his own eyes and let his thoughts drift, savoring the tranquility and hoping it would last.

But it didn't.

Chapter Fifteen

A faint trace of light tinged the eastern horizon when Nate awoke. He blinked a few times before he recalled where he was and the circumstances that had brought him to the top of the gorge. Rising, he stretched and went to relieve himself, then returned and gently shook the Crow woman.

Evening Star came awake instantly and glanced up. She nodded and went about rousing her daughter.

"Do you want food?" Nate asked.

"We will wait until midday," Evening Star responded.

"I can shoot something for breakfast."

"No. We should leave before the Utes come. But thank you for the offer."

"The Utes are not coming," Nate assured her, and headed for the horses. He halted when he heard a peculiar soft patter arising in the gorge. It couldn't be, he told himself, and ran to the rim to listen. Amplified by the rock walls, soft and inaudible at times but nonetheless recognizable, was the dull thud of horse hooves striking the gravel floor. He whirled and motioned for Evening Star to mount.

"The Utes?"

Nate frowned. "You were right."

"You killed two of the war party. They will chase us until they do the same to you and recapture us, or until all of them are dead."

So much for the Utes having an exaggerated reputation, Nate reflected, and quickly climbed onto the stallion. Once the mother and daughter were on the mare, he lead the pack animal off to the northwest, entering a verdant forest carpeted with pine needles. He reasoned that the Utes must have been tracking them all night since the band was already in the gorge. Once the war party found the spot where they had slept, the Indians would pick up the pace in the expectation of catching them soon.

Nate rode as fast as he dared, constantly avoiding trees and boulders, and whenever he came to a knoll or hill he would look back to see if there was sign of pursuit. Gradually the sun climbed into the sky, bringing the woodland to life, and with it came a steady rise in temperature.

Two hours after the sun rose Nate was perspiring freely. The day promised to be very warm, which meant they must locate water if they intended to push their animals to the limit. But although he scoured the terrain ceaselessly, none of the precious liquid was to be found.

In four hours the ground slanted downward into a broad valley, and in the center a small lake sparkled invitingly. Nate pointed at it and smiled, and Evening Star nodded happily. They pressed on until they broke from cover and saw the shore ahead, then galloped to the water's edge.

A flock of ducks was disturbed by their arrival, and across the lake a herd of deer moved warily off into the undergrowth.

Nate let the horses and the Crows slake their thirst first. When it was his turn, he dropped to his hands and knees and drank until he couldn't hold another drop. He straightened, smacked his lips, and wiped the back of his sleeve across his mouth.

"Do you think it is safe to stop for a while?" Evening Star inquired.

Turning, Nate surveyed the woods and hills they'd traversed. "There is no sign of the Utes yet. Yes, we can rest for a spell."

"I saw raspberry bushes over there," Evening Star signed, and pointed to the south. "If you will watch Laughing Eyes, I will collect them."

"Go ahead."

The Crow spoke a few stern words to her daughter, then ran off. Laughing Eyes gazed up at him, nervousness mirrored in her young eyes.

"You are safe with me," Nate promised her.

An uncomfortable silence ensued. The girl seemed transformed to stone, her gaze locked on his face.

Self-conscious under the child's scrutiny, Nate tried to initiate a conversation. "You are very mature for your age. I hope my own children turn out like you."

Laughing Eyes did not reply.

"Soon we will have you back with your father. Would you like that?"

At last the girl responded, her hands moving tentatively. "Yes."

"He will be very happy to see you," Nate predicted.

"I will be very sad."

"Why?"

"Because both my brothers are dead. I loved them with all my heart, and now I can never play with them again."

"They were good boys," Nate acknowledged sorrowfully.

"I hope my mother and father have another son one day so I can have a brother again."

"Maybe they will."

Silence descended once more. Nate didn't know what else to say. No amount of soothing words would alleviate the girl's suffering, and he'd rather keep quiet than remind her of the calamity. He squatted and splashed water on his throat and the back of his neck, then stood and watched their back trail.

Evening Star returned within minutes, her forearms cupped to her stomach and brimming with luscious red raspberries. She deposited them on the grass and smiled. "I can get more if you want."

"I am not very hungry," Nate said. "The two of you eat your fill." He stood guard while they crammed berries into their mouths, grinning as juice dribbled down Laughing Eye's pointed chin. Every now and then he bent down and grabbed a few berries for himself, and it was as he straightened for the fifth time that he saw the tendrils of dust rising approximately a quarter of a mile away. Shoving the raspberries in his mouth, he glanced at Evening Star. "The Utes."

She looked and stood. "We must leave immediately."

In a minute they were mounted and riding along the western shore of the lake. Nate cut into the trees when they came to a rocky stretch of ground that would make their tracks harder to read, then resumed their original northwesterly bearing, driving the horses even harder than before, sweating more than previously as the temperature climbed higher.

When they arrived at the north end of the valley they ascended a hill and paused to gaze at the lake. Visible on the west shore were seven riders.

The sight spurred Nate onward with a vengeance. Despite his best efforts, the war party would catch them by nightfall unless he came up with a ruse to throw the Utes off the scent. But what? How could he lose men who had demonstrated the ability to track at night? Doubling back was out of the question; it would put them behind the band and increase the jeopardy. A mile or two of solid stone underfoot would do the trick, but the woodland soil was essentially soft except for small tracks here and there. He toyed with the notion of an ambush to even the odds, and pondered whether he could prevail on the Crow to ride ahead without him.

Evening Star rode up alongside the stallion. Her daughter now sat behind her, arms looped about her waist. She caught Nate's attention and motioned while holding the reins. "There is a trick the Crows use to fool the Utes that might help us."

"What trick?"

"If we drag a limb behind us, our tracks will be erased. An excellent tracker would still be able to follow, but it would slow him down."

"It is a great idea," Nate signed, and reined up. He swiftly jumped down and used his knife to chop a thin, long branch sporting an abundance of leaves from a cottonwood. Next came the matter of a rope, which they didn't have.

Evening Star slid to the ground. "Give me your knife," she said, and extended her right hand.

Puzzled, Nate complied, and stared after her as she walked into the brush until she was out of sight. He smiled up at Laughing Eyes, who sat stiffly on the mare, and waited anxiously for the woman to return.

When Evening Star did step out, her dress was several inches shorter. She'd cut a continuous strip off the bottom hem of her dress, producing a tough buckskin strand ten feet in length. She beamed as he gave it to him.

Nate tied one end of the makeshift rope to the base of the branch, wrapped the other end around his left hand, and climbed into the saddle. "You will have to take the pack animal," he advised Evening Star.

She mounted the mare, took the lead, and rode forward.

Following on the pack animal's heels, Nate sat sideways so he could guide the path of the branch and ensure their prints were completely obliterated. He found that by moving his hand from side to side, the branch moved in a corresponding manner and effectively wiped the earth clean. Their deeper tracks were still imbedded in the soil, but even those were covered with a layer of needles, bits of vegetation, and dirt.

For half an hour they continued in such a manner, until the leaves on the branch were worn off by the friction and Nate had to halt to prepare a second limb. In no time they were on the move.

The blistering afternoon sun arced across the sky, and the shadows in the forest lengthened. Many small animals darted from their path and larger ones regarded them in curiosity. All went well until they came to a severely steep bald mountain.

Nate saw it first and realized the drawbacks it posed. Not only was the slope at an angle that would drastically slow the horses down, but the absence of trees and brush meant they would be visible for miles, exposed to the Utes. They might as well paint a sign announcing where they were. Rather than be foolish, they had to go around.

Evening Star bore to the left.

For no logical reason Nate felt inclined to bear to the right, but since she had already turned he acquiesced to her decision. The going became difficult, with numerous large boulders blocking the route, although the trees thinned out, which compensated somewhat. When the leaves on the second branch rubbed off, Nate reeled in the buckskin and placed it in his ammo pouch to use later. They'd traveled about two miles while covering their trail, and he figured that was enough to slow up the war party.

As they swung around the mountain a new vista unraveled before their eyes, a series of a dozen or so hills, each higher than the one before, most densely forested.

Nate was elated. There would be plenty of game and undoubtedly water, and with night approaching they needed both. If he constructed a lean-to, he could justify the risk of building a fire. A troubling notion occurred to him, giving him second thoughts. What if the Utes tracked them into the night? If so, the band would over-take them in the early hours of the morning before the sun rose. He had to weigh the benefits of stopping with the possible consequences.

Shortly they completed skirting the bald mountain and rode onto the nearest hill, where again a cushion of pine needles and leaves deadened the footfalls of their animals.

Nate decided to take the lead, and had started to swing around the other horses when the wilderness demonstrated once again why a person couldn't let down his guard for an instant. He heard loud barks off to the left and glanced in that direction.

Speeding toward them was a pack of wolves.

Chapter Sixteen

There were ten big gray wolves in all, their powerful forms flowing over the ground in rhythmic bounds, their reddish-pink tongues hanging out of their mouths, their sturdy teeth exposed. Standing close to three feet high at the shoulders and over six feet in length, they packed upwards of 130 pounds of sinew and muscle on their sleek frames. Individually, each wolf was formidable; together, they were terrors.

"Go!" Nate shouted at Evening Star, who had seen the pack and was already galloping away. He rode on her left side, intending to take the brunt of the assault if the wolves closed. All that he had ever learned about wolves came back to him in a twinkling; they were fast runners, tenacious hunters, and social animals who mated for life and were devoted to their offspring. Wolves normally avoided humans, although there were reports of attacks against trappers on record. Ordinarily hunting at night, they could be found abroad at any hour of the day if hunger drove them from their lairs.

The pack loped in pursuit, the leader 30 yards distant.

Should he fire to discourage them? Nate mused, and opted to hold off shooting until there was no alternative. A gunshot would give away their location to the Utes, and might serve to spark the band to intensify their efforts.

They crossed the crown and started down the opposite slope, the horses maintaining a steady gait. Evening Star rode easily, her daughter clinging tightly to her waist, proving that some Indian women were the equal of the men in horsemanship.

Nate noticed the wolves were not making a concerted attempt to overtake the horses, but were racing at a steady pace, and he reckoned the pack might be trying to tire the horses out before closing in. He scanned the countryside ahead and spied a creek that bisected the next hill halfway up.

Evening Star glanced back once as she neared the creek, her resolve transparent, all of her maternal instincts aroused by the potential threat to her child. She never bothered to slow down when she drew close to the bank. Undaunted, she plunged right in, the mare dutifully obedient to her prompting.

When Nate reached the bank, he halted. The wolves hadn't gained more than a yard or two, and now they cut back to a walk. The male leader suddenly stopped and sat on its haunches.

Unaware of this, Evening Star prodded the mare to the far bank 15 feet away, the water rising to the animal's chest, laboriously hauling the pack animal across.

All of the wolves had halted.

Nate realized the pack wasn't going to attack. The wolves must have given chase out of curiosity, not impelled by hunger. He'd heard about wolves that had trailed men for hours without displaying any hostility, which invariably mystified those nervous unfortunates who were the object of the wolves' attention. He rode across the creek and joined the woman and child. "I do not believe they will attack us," he signed.

"Apparently not," Evening Star replied, "but one never knows with wolves."

Nate gave a cheery wave at the pack, took the pack animal's lead from her, and began to head out. After the scare of the chase, his relief was all the more intense, and in the flush of relief he almost made a blunder. Jerking on the reins, he drew up short and glanced at the gently flowing water. The creek was ten feet across, and did not appear to be in any respect treacherous. He looked at his companions. "I have an idea. We should follow the creek for a few miles and slow the Utes down even more."

Evening Star seemed puzzled. "Along the bank? What good would that do?"

"Not along the bank. In the water."

Comprehension dawned and Evening Star smiled. "I should have thought of that."

Nate led off, moving to the middle of the flow, taking a northerly bearing. They would swing around to the northwest again later. He smiled at his cleverness, certain even the most proficient tracker in the world couldn't trail prints through water. The creek was crystal clear, and he could see every stone and pebble on the bottom as well as the many fish that flitted out of the stallion's path. He wished he could afford to take the time to catch a few for supper. Perhaps later, if all went well.

They pushed on until the sun touched the western horizon. The creek adhered to a generally northerly course the entire time, curving from time to time as it wound among the hills and mountains. Over a dozen times they startled big game drinking at the water's edge: buffalo, elk, deer, and a few black bear. Once they saw a panther that snarled at them before leaping off.

A cool breeze stroked Nate's brow and alleviated the heat. He spied a clearing up ahead on the left side and twisted in the saddle. "I propose to spend the night there," he told her, and indicated the spot.

"Good. Laughing Eyes needs rest badly."

"How are you holding up?"

"Well," Evening Star said, but the fatigue etched in her face belied her statement.

Nate gazed back along the winding watercourse. "Do you think the Utes have given up by now?"

"No."

"Why not? Between dragging the branch and following this creek, we are bound to have lost them."

"They will not give up because they are Utes."

"I still think we are safe."

"You thought that once before."

Having no retort for her astute observation, and troubled by the implications, Nate rode to the clearing and gladly climbed down. He tied the stallion and the pack horse to a tree, did the same with the mare, and walked into the trees to gather an armful of straight limbs for use in a lean-to.

"What are you doing?" Evening Star inquired when he emerged.

Nate dropped the load at his feet. "I will build a lean-to and a fire for tonight."

"Starting a fire is not wise. The Utes will see the smoke."

"Not if we build the fire *inside* the lean-to and keep the flames low. We will be able to cook and have enough warmth so we can sleep comfortably."

"But it is a great risk. If any of the smoke rises, the Utes will know where to find us."

Nate pointed at the little girl. "Do you want your child to go through another night without a hot meal and a comfortable place to sleep?"

Evening Star stared fondly at her offspring, and frowned. "No."

"Neither do I. I say we take the chance and build a fire, but I will forget all about the idea if you object."

"Go ahead."

With her helping him, Nate had a serviceable lean-to constructed before the sun dipped from sight. He rubbed his hands together, removing bits of bark and dirt, and gazed at the gradually darkening sky. "We will wait to build the fire until the sun is completely gone. That way, even if some smoke does escape, I doubt that the Utes will spot it. In the meantime, I must catch something for our meal."

"What will you catch? If you use your gun to kill game the Utes might hear."

Nate nodded at the creek. "I could catch fish for our meal."

"My people do not eat fish."

"I know, and under normal circumstances, I would not think of asking you to go against your beliefs. But the fish are handy and I can catch them without firing a shot." Nate glanced ar the child. "Laughing Eyes must be very hungry."

Evening Star looked at her daughter, her brow knit, the corners of her mouth curled downward as she wrestled with the dilemma of whether to violate the tribal taboo. At length she sighed and signed, "I would rather have my child eat than go hungry. If we must eat fish, we must."

"Are you sure?"

She locked her eyes on his. "My daughter is more important than our beliefs. I will live with the shame."

"All right. Stay on the bank and watch." Nate walked into the creek and moved slowly outward, bent at the waist, searching the bottom, trying to recall every aspect of the lessons Shakespeare had imparted in the finer art of fish catching. He saw a large whitefish swimming slowly toward him and crouched, oblivious of the water soaking his clothes and swirling about his legs. He slid his arms under the surface all the way to the shoulders, keeping his hands flat, the palms up, and waited expectantly. Fish were incredibly quick, and trying to hold onto their struggling, scaly bodies was like trying to hold onto a pig coated with grease—next to impossible. The secret to catching fish with bare hands was not to grip them, but to *flip* them.

The fish glided nearer.

Nate tensed, hoping the fish thought he was a rock, and when it started to swim over his hands he surged upward, clamping his fingers on the creature's slippery side as he swept his arms up and out. He couldn't quite believe his eyes when the fish sailed through the air and plopped onto the grass within a foot of the water. He'd done it! Elated, he dashed to the bank and scrambled out to prevent the fish from flopping back into the creek. He attempted to grab it but the fish popped from his grasp. Again and again he tried, each time with the same result. At last he succeeded in holding fast and glanced up in astonishment at hearing airy laughter.

Laughing Eyes was in hysterics. She spoke a few words to her mother between cackles.

"She says you are the funniest man alive," Evening Star translated, gazing at Nate affectionately.

"The fish are responsible for that."

Holding her sides, the girl laughed and laughed.

Evening Star chuckled. "Thank you," she signed, and gently touched his left cheek. "I was beginning to think she would never laugh again."

The comment caused Nate to recall the deaths of the boys, and brought to mind a revolting custom practiced by many of the Rocky Mountain tribes. Whenever a person lost a family member, the mourner engaged in an act of self-mutilation by hacking off part of a finger. His own wife had done so, and he now wondered if Evening Star would do the same.

"Is something wrong?" she inquired.

"No."

"What were you thinking about?"

Nate hesitated, then decided there was no reason to conceal the thought, although he rephrased it. "I am glad you did not cut off the tips of your fingers. You show good sense. The practice is barbaric and should be abolished by all Indians."

Evening Star's face clouded and she stared at her hands. "I am sorry you feel that way, because as soon as we return to the lodge I will slice off the tips of two fingers to mourn the passing of Strong Wolf and Red Hawk."

"Do you realize what you are doing?"

"Certainly. My people have always done this, since the days of the very first human beings. When a loved one dies, it is appropriate to express our grief in a fitting manner. By cutting off parts of our fingers, we prove the depth of our love and express our loss."

"Why not just cry your grief out?"

"Because crying does not show how deeply we loved those who died. People cry when a favorite horse is killed in a buffalo hunt, or when they have been injured and are in great pain. There is nothing special about crying. To demonstrate how special a loved one was, we must sacrifice a small part of ourselves."

"But why cut off a finger? Why not just jab yourself a few times with a knife or hold a burning coal in your palm?"

Evening Star shrugged. "It is our way. It has always been our way, and it always will be."

"I will never slice off part of my fingers," Nate vowed.

"Even if your wife were to die?"

"I would mourn her, yes, and I would miss her terribly, but I would not take a knife to my hand."

"If you become as we are, then you will."

Nate snorted at the idea. "I like the Indian way of life, but do not expect me to embrace every Indian custom. If Winona ever passes on, I will settle for crying many, many times."

"You never know," the woman said enigmatically.

"I know," Nate assured her. He went back into the creek, and in due course caught five more fine mountain whitefish.

Evening Star volunteered to clean the fish, but she grimaced as she hacked off the heads and removed the entrails.

The sun was gone by the time Nate got around to starting a fire in the lean-to. He carefully arranged the tinder and a circle of twigs and small branches in the middle of a ring of rocks, and once the flames took, he nursed it until he had a fair-sized fire going.

Stars filled the heavens and night enshrouded the land.

Evening Star handled the cooking. She rolled three large, flat stones into the heart of the flames, then removed them when they glowed red, using a stick to align them in a row. Placing a cleaned fish on each one, she hovered over the meal as the fish hissed and crackled.

Nate savored the tasty aroma. He walked to a pine tree and pried off sections of bark to use as plates, then returned. The girl was practically drooling on the fish, her eyes fixed hungrily on the sizzling morsels.

All in all, Nate decided, the day had gone well. They'd eluded the war party and had likely thrown the Utes off the scent. Although they'd swung wide of their original course, they would still be at the lodge by dark tomorrow. Once they arrived, he'd prevail on Sitting Bear to pack up the lodge and get the hell out of there.

Evening Star deftly flipped the fish over using twigs. A few stray wisps of smoke curled around the edges of the lean-to, but for the most part the smoke was blocked by the shelter and dissipated at ground level by the breeze.

Nate leaned back, feeling relaxed and content, and consequently he was unprepared for the loud whinnying of the stallion and the splashing sounds made by something or someone that was coming up the creek directly toward them.

Chapter Seventeen

Nate surged to his feet, the Hawken in his hands, and swung to the south in time to see a pair of Utes round the last curve at a gallop. At the sight of the lean-to they screeched and charged, one of the warriors waving a lance while the other nocked an arrow to a stout bow. Bewildered by their unexpected arrival, Nate took a second to recover from his shock.

Laughing Eyes threw her arms around her mother and whined pitiably.

The Ute with the bow took aim.

It was the thought of an arrow tearing into his chest that made Nate whip the rifle to his shoulder, take a hasty bead on the bowman, and fire. Simultaneously the Indian released the shaft, and both the ball and the arrow sped toward their respective targets at speeds too great for the eye to follow.

The ball took the warrior in the head and catapulted him from his mount. He fell into the creek with a splash.

A fraction of an instant later the arrow speared out of the night and streaked past Nate, narrowly missing his left side, to thud into the lean-to behind him. In order to protect the Crows better, he discarded the Hawken, drew both pistols, and ran to meet the second Ute head-on.

Throwing off a spray of water that seemed to sparkle in the moonlight, the warrior's horse made straight at Nate. The Ute arched his spine and drew back his lance, his features contorted in feral hatred.

Nate was almost to the bank when he pointed both flintlocks, cocked them, and stroked both triggers, the twin retorts booming as one, discharging small clouds of smoke, the recoil snapping his forearms upward.

Struck high in the chest by the balls just as he swept his arm forward, the Ute was lifted off his steed and sailed a good eight feet before he crashed into the water. His horse instantly swerved to the right and kept running until it disappeared in the blanket of darkness.

"Damn!" Nate swore, staring at the crumpled figures bobbing in the creek. Once again he'd misjudged the tenacity of the Utes. Their reputation for savagery, as he was learning to his sorrow, was, if anything, understated. He spun and marched back to the lean-to, where Evening Star and Laughing Eyes awaited him with tense expressions.

"The rest will be after us now," the mother signed. "Your shots have let them know where to find us."

Nate nodded and devoted himself to reloading all three guns, reflecting on their predicament as he did. The way he figured it, the Utes must have tracked them to the creek, at which point the band lost the trail, and then separated. Some of the warriors must have gone north along the watercourse, others south, and maybe a few had continued to the northwest just in case. If his calculations were correct, there were five warriors left and one of those was the one wounded by Strong Wolf.

"I will get the horses ready," Evening Star volunteered.

Nate glanced at the fish simmering on the stones and interrupted reloading to respond. "Eat first."

"We do not have time for food. The Utes are coming."

"For all we know they are miles in the other direction. It may take them a couple of hours to get here. And after all the trouble we've gone to preparing a decent meal, we are going to take a short time and enjoy the food," Nate said, and added for good measure. "Think of your daughter. She needs to eat to keep her strength up."

With obvious reluctance, Evening Star accepted his argument and knelt by the stones. She used her fingers to break the fish into bite-sized pieces and gave several to Laughing Eyes, then dug in herself.

Nate finished with the rifle and pistols and helped himself to a hot handful of delicious fish, his mouth watering at he took his first bite of the tasty, succulent meat. He was famished, and he consumed his fair share of the whitefish in no time. He even licked each of his fingers and his thumb when he was done, and smacked his lips in satisfaction. "The best fish I have ever eaten," he remarked.

"Fish *is* very tasty," Evening Star signed in amazement.

Laughing Eyes merely grinned from ear to ear, tiny bits of fish sticking to her chin.

"Now we can leave," Nate proposed.

"I will get the horses," Evening Star said, and walked off with the child in tow.

Nate put out the fire. He tore out a clump of long weeds, soaked them in the creek, and deposited the dripping vegetation on the flames, which sputtered and hissed and gave off lots of smoke. He tramped down hard repeatedly, stamping the fire out, and when there were no burning embers in evidence he moved to the horses.

Evening Star was already on the mare, Laughing Eyes behind her. She moved her arms slowly so he could read them in the gloom. "Will we go up the creek?"

"No. Since they know our approximate location, we might as well head directly for your lodge. If we ride all night we can be there by daylight."

"I like your plan. I am very worried about my husband."

Nate swung onto the stallion, took the lead to the packhorse in his left hand, and headed out, entering the dank, shadowy forest. Many of the big predators, like panthers and grizzlies, were more active at night, so he was extra alert as he rode on a beeline to the lodge. At least it was cool, which made the riding comfortable, and he liked the feel of the soft breeze on his face. After traveling for about half an hour they came to a clearing and he reined up to check his bearings, using the North Star as a guide.

Once Nate was convinced they were on the

right course, he pushed on as fast as the benighted conditions warranted, the Hawken resting across his thighs. The minutes became hours as they forged steadily onward, crossing hills and valleys, skirting the high peaks and the deep ravines, traversing several streams and passing another lake.

Nate listened for sounds of pursuit, but none materialized. Her periodically fought off bouts of drowsiness, and once almost dozed off in the saddle. The tip of a branch gouged him in the cheek, snapping him erect, and he shook his head vigorously to clear out the cobwebs.

Evening Star and Laughing Eyes rode silently, unable to communicate with him because of the gloom.

As the night wore on, the ride acquired a degree of monotony that Nate found oddly reassuring. Every mile they went without being attacked increased the likelihood they would reach Sitting Bear without further incident. He hoped the warrior was resting, as he'd suggested.

Occasionally an owl hooted in the trees. Wolves howled frequently. Crickets chirped all around them.

Nate kept scouring the countryside ahead for a landmark he might recognize, such as a familiar mountain, but the terrain was alien at night, an inky expanse stretching into infinity.

At one point, as they were passing through a particularly dense track of woodland, an ominous, throaty growl pierced the air from a thicket off to their right, and the entire thicket shook and rattled as if alive. Finally they heard a huge beast crash through the undergrowth, heading to the north.

Slowly the positions of the stars shifted

minutely as the night waned, and eventually a faint tinge of light graced the rim of sky to the east.

Nate was beginning to think he'd misjudged the bearing when they rode out of yet another stretch of forest, and there, not 15 yards in front of them, was the stream he'd followed to the southeast, the same stream that ran past Sitting Bear's lodge. He reined up in surprise, then looked at Evening Star, and they both beamed. Advancing to the bank, he scanned in both directions, and concluded they weren't more than two or three miles from the camp.

With a happy heart Nate turned to the northwest and hastened along the east bank. They had gone a mile when the stallion suddenly snorted and acted up, its ears pricked, its eyes on the trees to the west. Nate stopped and listened but heard no unusual sounds, so he urged the big black on.

Evening Star brought the mare alongside the stallion as they neared the vicinity of her home. Her daughter was slumped against her back, swaying with every step, asleep.

Nate thought of how delighted Sitting Bear would be to have his wife and daughter safely returned, a joyous reunion they would never forget, and complimented himself on a job well done. It felt good to have done something for others that would bring them such happiness, almost as if he'd contributed something mean-ingful to the scheme of existence. He'd never considered himself much of a philosopher, and had never attached much significance to his life, but at that moment he felt as if he'd justified his presence on the planet.

Dawn flushed the sky with striking hues of

pink, orange, and yellow by the time they drew close enough to spy the lodge. Smoke curled from the top and the front flap was open.

Evening Star laughed, reached back to wrap her left arm around Laughing Eyes, and broke into a gallop.

About to do the same, Nate abruptly changed his mind. The husband and wife would probably desire a few moments of privacy. He slowed up and absently gazed at the trees and the sky, enjoying the unfolding of a new day.

Halting near the teepees, Evening Star slid to the ground, took her daughter into her arms, and hastened inside, calling out as she did so.

Nate saw the other two horses he'd brought back munching on grass at the edge of the field near the trees, which assured him no Utes had been there since his departure.

Suddenly mother and daughter burst from the lodge and Evening Star motioned excitedly for him to come over.

Puzzled, Nate complied, sliding off the stallion almost at her feet. "What is it?" he asked.

"Sitting Bear is missing."

Nate glanced at the doorway. "He is not in there?"

"No," Evening Star said, and apprehensively scanned their surroundings.

"He has to be here somewhere," Nate assured her. "Maybe he went for a walk." Deep down, though, he doubted his own explanation, and he moved toward the stream while scouring the landscape for the warrior. Since the fire in the lodge was still going, Sitting Bear couldn't have gone very far. He probed the woods to the rear, then the field, and finally the stream.

Off the the left, partly concealed in thick weeds on the bank, was a prone form.

"Evening Star!" Nate called out, forgetting himself, and dashed to the water. There lay Sitting Bear, unconscious, his forearms dangling in the stream. Kneeling, Nate pulled the Crow higher and rolled him over. He felt as if he'd grabbed a burning torch in his hands.

In a twinkling Evening Star was there, examining her husband carefully, her countenance mirroring her anxiety. "He has an extremely high fever," she reported. "We must get him inside right away."

"Take my rifle," Nate signed, and gave the Hawken to her. He lifted the warrior and hurried into the lodge to deposit Sitting Bear near the fire. No sooner did he straighten up than his rifle was back in his hands and the woman was tending to her husband.

Laughing Eyes sat nearby, watching intently.

"Is there anything I can do?" Nate asked.

"Do you know how to recognize herbs?"

"No."

"Then watch my daughter while I get the medicine Sitting Bear needs," Evening Star suggested, and dashed out before he could respond.

Nate smiled encouragement at the child and took a seat. He noticed a stack of broken branches, and fed a few to the fingers of flame simply to keep busy. So much for his great plan to leave right away. If they tried to move Sitting Bear in his weakened state, the man would surely die. They were stuck there until the Crow recovered sufficiently to travel, which could take days and meant the Utes would easily overtake them.

The Utes.

He stared at the doorway, reflecting. If the war party was eliminated, so was the danger. But how could he hope to defeat five Utes by himself? So far he'd been lucky, and luck was a fickle ally to rely on. Despondent over the turn of events, he absently gazed at Sitting Bear and blinked in surprise.

The Crow's eyes were open.

Chapter Eighteen

Nate promptly moved closer and smiled at his friend. "Stay right where you are," he directed.

Sitting Bear licked his lips, his eyelids fluttering, then recovered enough to feebly move his hands. "Evening Star and Laughing Eyes."

"They are here safe and sound."

The warrior craned his neck with great effort and saw his daughter. Smiling broadly, he spoke a few words to her.

Voicing a cry of joy, the child scrambled to her father's side and placed her head on his chest. Tears poured down her cheeks and she uttered soft sobs. Sitting Bear tenderly patted her head, then glanced at Nate. "Are the Utes all dead?"

"Five still live."

"They will follow you here."

"I know."

"Do you know what must be done?"

"Yes."

"There might be another way. If you hide us in the forest, perhaps they will not find us and will leave."

"You know better."

A slight nod signified the Crow's acknowledgment, and he closed his eyes, sighed, and passed out.

Nate let Laughing Eyes stay with her father. He rose, grabbed his Hawken, and moved to the doorway, where he crouched and surveyed the terrain to the southeast. When the Utes came, they would likely come from that direction. He saw no sign of them, but that didn't mean the war party wasn't out there, maybe five miles off, maybe ten.

A robin landed near the flap, saw him, and took wing again.

He was like that bird, he told himself. He couldn't afford to sit still when there was a threat to his existence, and that of his new friends, lurking in the background. Either they fled, which they couldn't do given the circumstances, or they made a fight of it. Or one of them did.

Nate was still pondering the inevitable when Evening Star returned bearing a selection of plants. She immediately went to Sitting Bear, and Nate watched her for a minute before slipping quietly out and making for the stallion. There was no sense in trying to explain his decision. She might argue, try to get him to change his mind, when there could be no turning back. Her ministrations would keep her too busy to notice his absence for a while, and he could ride off unnoticed. He was almost to the horse when he heard the patter of rushing feet and a hand fell on his right shoulder. Calmly, unwilling to show how nervous he really was, he turned and smiled. "You should be with Sitting Bear."

"Where do you think you are going?" Evening Star demanded.

"You know where," Nate told her.

Her eyes darted to the southeast and back again. "We can run. Let me tend my husband, and in an hour we can head for our village."

Nate took the liberty of affectionately touching her cheek, and shook his head. "You know better. Take good care of him. If I am not back by tomorrow morning, you should make a travois and get him and your daughter out of here. Understand?"

Evening Star simply nodded. Her eyes conveyed her feelings more than words ever could. Turning, she ran back to the lodge and disappeared within.

An odd wave of raw emotion engulfed him, and Nate coughed as he walked to the stallion and swung up. Jerking on the reins, he wheeled the animal and rode toward his rendezvous with five of the fiercest fighters in the Rockies. He recalled a certain spot they'd passed the night before, a narrow opening between two steep hills, that would admirably serve his purpose if he could reach it before the band.

Although fatigue gnawed at his mind and body, Nate galloped into the midst of the mountains again, stopping only once after two hours to take a drink from the stream. By the third hour he'd arrived at the site, and sat in the saddle while determining the best place to make his stand.

The two hills were devoid of vegetation and covered with rocks and boulders. Between them was the opening, ten yards at the widest and 30 yards in length, rimmed by scattered, isolated trees, a mix of cottonwoods and pines. He turned to the right and rode into the shadowed shelter of a boulder as big as a house, then dismounted and let the reins drag on the ground. If he needed to make a quick getaway, he didn't want to bother with untying them.

Nate jogged to the opening and halted behind the trunk of a cottonwood. His gaze roved over all the trees and depressions, seeking an ideal ambush point. None were outstanding, but there were three pines growing close to each other on the left side that would suffice. He moved behind them, estimating the boulder to be ten yards off, and crouched.

Now let the Utes come!

After confirming all three guns were loaded, he leaned his back against the trunk and plotted strategy. He wasn't a skilled military man, so he must rely on cunning instead of firepower. Even if he killed three of the war party with his first three shots, which was unlikely, the rest would be on him before he could reload. How could he slow them down?

Nate suddenly remembered the buckskin rope Evening Star had made, and reached into his ammo pouch. It wasn't the strongest rope ever made, but it was thin enough and long enough to do the trick. Rising, he stepped closer to the boulder and selected two cottonwoods spaced approximately nine feet apart. He shimmied up one, tied the rope at a level corresponding to the height of a man on horseback, then climbed down and repeated the procedure on the second tree. Once on firm footing, he regarded his handiwork critically. Anyone going slowly was bound to notice the trap, so it was up to him to make certain the Utes had no time to admire the scenery.

He walked to the pines and knelt, adjusted the pistols under his belt, and lifted the rifle. All was in readiness. Now all he could do was wait.

A jay landed in the tree overhead, voiced its

shrill cry a few times, and flew off.

Nate thought about Winona. She must be very worried about him, and he wouldn't blame her if she gave him a scolding when he finally made it back to their cabin. Knowing her as he did, he knew she'd probably simply hug him until his ribs cracked and whisper in his ears how much she'd missed him. Never had he felt so loved, never so happy, as when they began their married life. He leaned against the tree, ruminating.

The sun rose higher and higher into the blue vault of the sky.

Nate's rumbling stomach reminded him of his acute hunger, but he refused to leave his post to find food. The discomfort helped to keep him awake and alert. If he ate, he'd become too drowsy to keep his eyes open. He'd never gone this long without sleep before, and he didn't know how much longer he could hold up.

By noon his eyelids were drooping, his chin sagging. He slapped his cheek repeatedly to no avail. Shaking his head vigorously did nothing to stem the overwhelming tide of weariness. Frustrated, he heaved to his feet and swung his arms from side to side. He listened to the birds and the whispering breeze.

Suddenly, from the southeast, came the whinny of a horse.

Nate froze and stared through the opening at the woods beyond. He thought he detected movement far back under the trees and he squatted, now in full possession of his faculties. It had to be the Utes!

Soon a rider appeared, then another and another, alternately passing through shadows and beams of golden sunlight, sitting loosely astride their mounts.

Scarcely breathing, Nate molded his body to
the tree and peeked around the edge, exposing
as little of himself as possible. Now that the band
had finally arrived, it almost seemed like a
dream, as if he were detached from the proceed-
ings, an observer instead of a participant.

The first Ute carried a fusee, the second a bow,
the third a lance. The third man was the same
warrior wounded by Strong Wolf, still wearing
the crude bandage and swaying precariously
with every step his animal took. It seemed
doubtful he'd live out the day.

Nate kept the Hawken pressed flush with his
body. He saw the lead rider studying the ground,
and entertained the hope of catching the man
completely off guard. But as the Utes approached
the gap, the foremost warrior paid less attention
to the tracks he was following and more to the
terrain ahead.

The second warrior looked over his shoulder,
then halted and waited for the wounded man to
catch up. They exchanged words, then rode on
together.

An unexpected wave of dizziness assailed Nate,
and he had to close his eyes to steady himself.
The lack of sleep and food, plus the sustained
strain of the flight, was taking its toll. Not now!
he thought, and gazed at the Indians again.

When the lead rider reached the gap, he halted
and intently scrutinized the hills and the trees
for a few moments, as if he suspected something
was wrong but couldn't put his finger on it.
Holding the fusee in his left hand, he goaded his
animal into the opening.

A strange, troubling thought entered Nate's
mind: What if he was killed? Winona would never

know what had happened to him. His body would lie where it fell, slowly rotting, or be consumed by scavengers. He envisioned his scalped form, partly eaten and stinking to high heaven, lying in the dirt, and felt bile rise in his throat. The image sparked a fleeting terror, and he hesitated.

Ten yards into the gap, the first Ute watched a pair of doves take flight from a cottonwood.

Nate almost panicked, almost whipped the rifle up and fired prematurely. Realizing the consequences of such rash action brought him to his senses. He had to be calm, to keep his wits about him at all times. Waiting was the key to success. Wait. Wait. Wait.

The lead Ute drew within 20 feet of the three pines. He shifted and looked at his companions.

In that instant when the warrior's attention was diverted, Nate raised the Hawken to his shoulder, cocked the hammer, and took careful aim.

Both the wounded Indian and the warrior with the bow spotted him and cried out in warning.

Swiveling, the lead rider instinctively started to bring the fusee to bear while simultaneously diving to the right.

Nate had to compensate, tracking the Ute's body, and he rushed his shot, squeezing the trigger while the warrior was in midair. At the same instant the Ute cut loose with the fusee, and a burning sensation lanced through Nate's right shoulder. He'd been hit! Stunned, he staggered backwards, then dropped to his knees behind another tree.

The first Ute was on the ground and scurrying on his hands and knees toward his friends, who had reined up and were taking cover.

Looking at his shoulder, Nate was horrified to

see a tear in the buckskin and blood seeping out. He fought to get a grip on his nerves and resisted an impulse to flee. Yes, he'd been hit, but he was still alive, still able to fight. He gingerly probed the tear and discovered he'd sustained a flesh wound, nothing more. The ball wasn't imbedded. Relieved, he looked toward the Utes in time to observe the lead rider crawl behind a waist-high bush.

There was no sign of the other two.

Nate pulled his head back, rested his forehead on the bole, and took stock. His carelessness had cost him dearly. Not only had he ruined the element of surprise, but apparently he'd missed. There were three Indians out there somewhere, eager to slit his throat.

Hold on a second.

Why were there only three?

Perplexed, Nate straightened and began reloading. There should be five Utes left out of the original nine. What could have happened to the other two? Were they en route to the Ute village for reinforcements? Or were they farther back along the trail?

A peculiar trilling noise arose to the southwest.

In the act of feeding powder down the barrel, Nate paused and scanned the gap. That sound had been like no bird he'd ever heard, and he wondered if the Utes were trying to circle past him. Working swiftly, he finished pouring the powder, wrapped a ball in a patch and wedged both into the barrel using his thumb, then shoved both all the way down with the detachable ramrod. After sliding the rod into its housing, he was ready.

All the wildlife in the immediate vicinity had fallen silent, and the breeze had died down.

Since the Utes knew where he was, Nate decided to head elsewhere. He flattened and made toward a pine ten feet away, and once its trunk sheltered him he rose cautiously to his knees and risked another look-see. Still no trace of the warriors. He looked toward the bush where the first man had vanished and detected a crimson smear on the grass. Maybe he hadn't missed, after all.

A twig snapped to the right.

Pivoting, Nate spied one of his foes moving behind a boulder, proving they were trying to hem him in. He flattened again and retreated even farther, until he was lying at the base of a forked cottonwood and peering between the two trunks. Easing the Hawken out, he scoured the opening and the facing slopes.

Come on!

Show yourselves!

One of the Indians did, the man carrying the bow. He was creeping around the bottom of the boulder on the right, an arrow set to fly, his attention on the last pine.

This time Nate was determined not to miss. He sighted on the warrior's head, and he was just about to fire when he heard onrushing footfalls to his left attended by a strident screech of savage fury.

Chapter Nineteen

In the instant Nate had to react, he squeezed off the shot and rolled to the right, not bothering to see whether he'd scored or not, flipping onto his back and reaching for his pistols.

The first Ute was almost on him. A ball had struck the warrior in the lelft side, gouging a deep furrow in his flesh, and he had discarded the fusee in favor of a tomahawk that he arced at Nate's chest.

Desperately throwing himself to the left, Nate narrowly evaded the weapon. The tomahawk bit into the earth within inches of his ribs. He swept both flintlocks up and out, certain of slaying his adversary before the Ute could swing again, only the warrior pounced instead of swinging, batting Nate's arms aside and landing on his chest.

Whooping lustily, the Ute raised the tomahawk for another blow.

There was no time to shoot. Nate elevated the right pistol and deftly deflected the tomahawk as it drove toward his face, then smashed the left flintlock into the man's cheek, sending him sprawling. Surging to his feet, he tried to extend both pistols and fire, but the warrior, still on the ground, kicked Nate's legs out from under him and he fell onto his back.

The tomahawk descended toward his face.

Nate rolled, and heard the thud as the sharpened edge hit the soil where his head had just been. He scrambled to his knees and twisted, and there was the warrior lunging at him, the tomahawk uplifted once more. In reflex he pointed the right pistol and sent a ball into his face.

Because of the angle, the shot took the Ute squarely in the throat and rocked him backwards. A red geyser gushed from his severed veins, but that didn't stop him from trying to wield the tomahawk yet one more time. Gurgling, he coiled to spring.

Firing from the hip, Nate delivered a ball to the warrior's forehead that slammed the man rearward. Discarding the right flintlock, he drew his knife, prepared to close if necessary.

The Ute wouldn't attack any more trappers. He was limp, on his back, his eyes wide and lifeless.

For a second Nate stared at his vanquished enemy, amazed he had triumphed, and then he remembered there were other warriors eager to take his scalp. He dropped down, stuck the one pistol under his belt and retrieved the other, then crawled to his rifle.

An unnatural silence gripped the wilderness.

Nate glanced at the boulder, and nearly shouted for joy at spying the bowman dead at its base. Two down and one to go, and that one was wounded! He set about reloading all three guns, starting with the Hawken, and he was tugging on the ramrod to extract it when the heavy pounding of hooves sounded and a defiant cry rent the air. Startled, he glanced up.

The third Ute intended to go out fighting. Despite his wound—or was it because of it?— the warrior had remounted and now galloped forward, the lance upraised, grim determination etching his visage.

Letting the rifle drop, Nate clutched the knife and stood, using the right fork for cover, aware that a misstep would cost his life. Neither of the cottonwood forks were wide enough to conceal him entirely; he'd have to dodge at the very instant the lance was hurled.

The Ute's eyes had a crazed aspect. He sneered and rode right up to the cottonwoods, apparently aware the rifle and pistols were expended.

Nate tensed, and saw the lance tip sweep at his head. He shifted, keeping the trunk between them, but he shifted too far and exposed himself on the other side. Again the lance stabbed out, and he barely skipped backwards out of range.

Laughing harshly, the warrior expertly maneuvered his horse so he could strike between the forks.

Nate darted to the right, racking his brain for a way to turn the tables. If he stayed where he was, eventually the Ute would connect. A knife was no match for a spear. There had to be a better way.

"Bastard!" the Ute barked, and struck.

So surprised was Nate at hearing English spoken by his foe, that he stood there for a fraction of a second in shock. The lance was within inches of his chest when he frantically twisted and glided to the right, the razor tip tearing through his buckskin shirt and slicing a furrow in his chest.

The warrior whooped.

And suddenly Nate knew what he had to do. All trace of fear was gone, supplanted by a firm resolve to win at all costs. He whirled and ran, but not at his top speed, and glanced over his right shoulder.

Predictably, the Ute took the bait, goading his mount around the cottonwood tree and giving chase.

"Fish-eater!" Nate yelled, his legs pumping, ignoring the intense stinging sensation in his chest, heading toward the boulder, deliberately holding back until the proper moment.

Elevating the lance, the warrior rapidly covered the ground. A grin betrayed his confidence. He thought he had the white man right where he wanted him.

Nate looked at the pair of trees, then at the Ute. It would be close. He ran faster, his heart thumping, his temples throbbing, caked with sweat. Just a few more feet! That was all he needed. The drumming hooves seemed to be almost on top of him when he passed under the buckskin rope, and he leaped to the right as he glanced at his enemy.

The Ute rode straight into the trap. Rabidly intent on throwing his lance into the hated white's back, he concentrated on his running quarry to the exclusion of all else. The makeshift rope caught him a few inches below the neck and lifted him clean off his steed to topple hard onto his back, the lance flying from his hand.

The thought of taking a prisoner or sparing the warrior never entered Nate's mind. He sprang, alighting on top of the Ute and plunging his knife into the man's chest in the same motion. Once, twice, three times he buried the butcher knife to the hilt, and with each blow the warrior bucked and hissed.

Abruptly, the Ute gasped, thrashed feebly, and expired.

Taking a deep breath, Nate slowly rose, his eyes on the warrior's. He'd won. He'd actually won. Oddly, he didn't feel elated, didn't feel pleased with himself. How could he when he'd just slain three men? Three more to add to the total. What *was* the total so far? He'd honestly forgotten.

Did it even matter?

He took several wobbly strides, the excitement making him giddy. At least Sitting Bear, Evening Star, and Laughing Eyes were safe. He'd repaid them for their kindness and generosity. All he had to do was see them safely to their village, and he could hasten to his cabin and the lovely woman he longed to embrace.

The war party was finished.

Or was it?

Nate recalled there were still two members of the band unaccounted for, and he adhered to his earlier reasoning that the others must be scouring the countryside elsewhere or on their way to their own village. Who *cared* where they were? It didn't matter in the slightest.

Or did it?

A chilling thought instantly sobered him and prompted him to stare to the northwest in alarm. What if—and the idea was almost too horrible to contemplate—what if the remaining pair wasn't somewhere along the back trail? What if they had taken a different route and were in *front* of him? What if they'd taken a shortcut to the

Crow camp while the others had followed the tracks? That way, the Utes would have been assured of catching all of them.

Dear Lord!

Could it be?

A terrible premonition seized him, and he dashed to his guns. He fumbled with the powder and the balls as he reloaded the flintlocks and the rifle, and then he was sprinting to the stallion and vaulting into the saddle.

Please let him be wrong!

He jerked on the reins and brought the big black to a gallop, riding recklessly, the rifle in his left hand, forgetting all about his wounds, thinking only of the family he'd grown to care for, to love as if they were his very own.

The terrain flashed by. He lost all track of time, all track of the ground covered, all track of everything except his burning desire to reach the lodge as quickly as possible. When the stallion flagged, he urged it on, knowing the animal needed rest just as he did, knowing it had been through so much already, knowing it might die if he kept pushing, but push he did. The precious lives of the three Crows were more important than that of a horse, more important than his own. He'd vowed to protect them, and protect them he would, with his dying breath if need be.

Deer fled at his approach. Elk snorted and melted into the shadows. Buffalo regarded him warily.

Nate hardly noticed. His chest stung, his shoulder ached, his thighs were sore, his back stiff, but he cared not at all. All that counted was reaching the lodge.

The stallion was breathing heavily, its chest flecked with foam, its nostrils flaring, when they finally broke from the last stretch of forest and saw the field ahead. Nate's own breath caught in his throat when he spied the strange horses near the teepee and spied two men moving about near the doorway. An uncontrollable rage gripped every fiber of his being, a fury surpassing all furies, and he saw the world through a reddish haze. "No!" he screamed, and swept onward.

Both Utes were on their mounts in a flash, and together they wheeled and rode to meet him. One carried a bow, the other a war club.

Nate never swerved, never deviated from his course as he bore down on the warriors. He saw the bowman notch a shaft, but paid no heed. The Ute bearing the war club raised it on high, but he ignored that. All that mattered was protecting the Crows. All that counted was making sure the Utes never killed another innocent person. Even when the bowman aimed and let the arrow fly, he kept on charging.

The shaft streaked through the air, a lethal blur that no man could evade.

Nate didn't bother trying. His blood boiling, all he cared about was reaching the Utes. He glimpsed the shaft as it whizzed past his face, nicking his left cheek and drawing blood, and then he was almost upon them, still galloping all out. The Hawken molded to his right shoulder, he took a bead on the archer's head, and fired. Without waiting to observe the result, he angled the stallion at the second warrior, ramming the big black into the Ute's mount and bowling it over. The impact nearly unseated him, and then he saw the warrior struggling to rise, the man's leg pinned under the downed animal. He tossed the rifle aside, drew his knife, and vaulted from the saddle.

The Ute looked up and tried to bring the war club into play.

Nate landed on the Indian's horse as it tried to rise, sliding over its back to slam onto the warrior. His left hand grasped his foe's wrist, preventing the war club from swinging, even as the Ute grabbed his knife hand. The horse reached its feet, leaving them free to grapple and roll from side to side as each man strived to prevail.

As he glared into Nate's eyes, the Ute's countenance was transformed by sheer hatred into a feral mask.

Nate's fury lent strength to his arms. He ripped his hand loose and sank the knife into the warrior's side, not once but again and again and again, stabbing long after the Ute had ceased moving, long after his hand was coated with blood and red dots covered his shirt, neck, and chin. Only when a drop of blood sprayed onto his upper lip did he stop, suddenly aware of what he was doing, and lower his arm.

Feeling a singular numbness in his limbs, Nate rose awkwardly and shuffled a few feet from the Ute. He stared at the archer and found him dead in the high weeds. Belatedly, the shock hit, a reaction to the incensed combat. For a minute he stood still, striving to recover his senses. And then he remembered the Crows.

Evening Star!

Spinning, Nate ran toward the lodge, his gaze taking in the open flap and the lack of activity, as well as the absence of smoke. Please let them be all right, he prayed. Please let them be bound or staked out or hiding in the forest, but please let them be alive above all else! He slowed ten feet away. "Sitting Bear! Evening Star! Where are you?"

There was no answer.

Nate had to force his legs to take the necessary step to the lodge, and he was trembling when he sank to his knees and looked inside. A whine escaped his lips. He closed his eyes and groaned. "Oh God," he said softly, and doubled over, his arms wrapped around his midriff. The tears, when they came, wouldn't stop, and for the longest while the only sound that arose from the Crow camp were great, choking sobs.

Epilogue

The beautiful Indian woman with the flowing tresses and the troubled dark eyes were strolling along the south shore of a lake high in the Rockies, near a quaint cabin, when she happened to look to the west and spotted the lone rider. Instantly her hand flew to her mouth and her heart fluttered. She watched, scarcely believing her eyes, then broke into a run and shouted one of the few English words she knew. "Shakespeare! Shakespeare!"

From out of the cabin came a grizzled mountain man wearing buckskins and a brown beaver hat. He stared at her in bewilderment, then addressed her in the Shoshone tongue. "What is it, Winona? A grizzly?"

Winona gestured and exclaimed happily, "Nate! Nate!"

Pivoting, the mountain man let out a yell of delight. He waited for her to reach him, then they ran to meet her husband. "What did I tell you?" Shakespeare said. "I knew he'd come back safe and sound."

"Nate!" Winona shouted.

The solitary rider was leading a string of six horses. He gave a little wave and rode faster. Both the man and the animals appeared tremendously fatigued. When he reined up, he slid from the mare and seemed to sag. Straightening, he tossed his rifle to Shakespeare and opened his arms wide to embrace Winona.

His eyes narrowing, the mountain man studied the younger man's face. "You had us a bit worried. Where the hell have you been?"

Hugging his wife close, Nate stared over her shoulder at his mentor. "Took me a little longer than I figured. Sorry."

Shakespeare noted the haggard aspect of his friend's features and detected—something—in Nate's eyes, something that hadn't been there before he left. "Are you all right?"

"Yes."

"Another day and I would have lit out after you."

Nate didn't respond. He closed his eyes and inhaled the sweet fragrance of Winona's hair.

"What happened?"

"I don't want to talk about it."

The curt reply made Shakespeare pause. "Whatever you want, Nate. I didn't mean to pry." He turned and walked toward the cabin.

"Wait."

Shakespeare halted and looked back. "What is it? I thought I'd give you some time to yourselves."

"Are you on good terms with the Crows?"

Mystified by the unusual question, Shakespeare nodded.

"Do you know their top chief?"

"Chief Long Hair? Yep. Know him well. Why?"

"Do you know where he has his village this time of year?"

"Sure. Up near the Wind River," Shakespeare said. "Do you mind telling me what all this is about?"

Nate whispered a few words into Winona's ear, then released her. He stepped to his pack animal and removed a number of thin items from a pouch.

"What are those?" Shakespeare inquired.

"Eagle feathers," Nate said, extending his arm and opening his hand to reveal five feathers.

"What in the world are you doing with those?"

"After I've rested up, I want you to take me to Chief Long Hair's village. These feathers are for him." Nate motioned at the extra horses he'd brought back. "So are they."

Bewildered, the mountain man scratched his head and nodded. "Okay. If that's what you want. But I don't understand."

"I'll explain later," Nate promised. He took Winona's hand and headed toward their home. "Right now there's another favor you can do for me."

"Anything. You know that."

"Go for a ride."

"A ride?" Shakespeare repeated, and gazed at Winona's back. "Oh. Sure. At least I understand this request."

"Thanks. You have no idea how much this means to me."

Chuckling, Shakespeare stepped to the mare and took her reins. "Don't worry about the horses. I'll tend to them, then go for my little ride." He started to lead the animals toward the meadow bordering the cabin. "Say, how long do you want me to be gone, anyway?"

Nate answered without turning around. "Two or three days would be nice."

AUTHOR'S NOTE

Most people are familiar with the fact that at one time there was in widespread use among American Indians a medium of communication known as sign language. Combining hand movements and arm gestures, this universal language enabled Indians from different tribes, who ordinarily spoke quite distinct languages, to converse freely and easily. In 1885 it was estimated there were 110,000 sign-talking Indians in the U.S. Since then, with so many Native Americans enjoying the presumed benefits of a modern education, there are few left who can converse in sign.

In frontier times, when the first white men went West, many of them learned this language and used it extensively in their dealings with the Indians. Not until you read the actual accounts of trappers and mountain men do you realize just how widely this was done.

Certain liberties have been taken in this book to accommodate modern sentence construction because the proper sign sequence might cause confusion. For instance, the question "How old are you?" translated into sign becomes: *"Question-how-*

many-you-winter." Or take another example such as, "I feel very sad." In sign this becomes: *"I-heart-on-the-ground."* I hope historical purists will forgive me for conforming to current literary form.

Indian sign language is an effective, beautiful medium of expression, and it's unfortunate that sign is now relegated to the status of a relic from the past.